THE ANTAGONIST

by

Jonas Saul

PUBLISHED BY:
Imagine Press Inc.
Ebook ISBN: 978-1-927404-34-8
Paperback ISBN: 978-1-998047-09-3
Hardcover ISBN: 978-1-998047-32-1

The Antagonist
Copyright © 2014 by Jonas Saul

The Sarah Roberts Series

Dark Visions (One)
The Warning (Two)
The Crypt (Three)
The Hostage (Four)
The Victim (Five)
The Enigma (Six)
The Vigilante (Seven)
The Rogue (Eight)
Killing Sarah (Nine)
The Antagonist (Ten)
The Redeemed (Eleven)
The Haunted (Twelve)
The Unlucky (Thirteen)
The Abandoned (Fourteen)
The Cartel (Fifteen)
Losing Sarah (Sixteen)
The Pact (Seventeen)
The Terror (Eighteen)
The Chase (Nineteen)
The Betrayal (Twenty)
Sarah's Return (Twenty-One)
The Hunt (Twenty-Two)
The Delivery (Twenty-Three)
The Trap (Twenty-Four)
The Ultimatum (Twenty-Five)
The Depraved (Twenty-Six)
The Condemned (Twenty-Seven)
Payback (Twenty-Eight)
The Unknown (Twenty-Nine)
Wrath (Thirty)
The Damned (Thirty-One)
The Game (Thirty-Two)

Jonas Saul

The Decoy (Thirty-Three)
The Disappearance (Thirty-Four)
The Whole Truth (Thirty-Five)
Alex (Thirty-Six)
Parkman (Thirty-Seven)
Darwin (Thirty-Eight)
Aaron (Thirty-Nine)
Remains To Be Seen (Forty)

The Jake Wood Novels

The Immortal Gene (Book One)
The Immortal Target (Book Two)

Standalone Novels

'Til Death Do Us Part
The Drowning
The Woman in the Woods
The Threat
The Specter
The Mafia Trilogy
A Murder in Time
Frequency of the Dead

Co-Authored Novels

Collision Course (Written with Gary Ponzo)
There Will Be Blood (Written with Rania Stone)
The Soulless (Written with Rania Stone)

Short Story Collections

Twisted Fate (Tales of Horror)

The Antagonist

Twists of Fate (Tales of Hope)

Chapter 1

Sarah Roberts didn't want to antagonize the police without reason, but her sister's message was clear, and Sarah wasn't about to question Vivian.

Traffic on the William Bennet Bridge stood still in the early afternoon heat of August. Personal watercraft, jet-skis, and houseboats filled Lake Okanagan below, backed up behind a couple of police boats circling the area where a woman had just jumped off the bridge.

Lesley Wright, age thirty, despondent, depressed, and tired of her life, had stood on the edge of the bridge for an hour, then jumped.

Sarah had sat on her motorcycle behind a line of cars blocked from going forward until the police had rescued the woman. Twenty cars back from where the woman had jumped, Sarah watched as the RCMP attempted to negotiate Lesley back from the edge. Half a minute ago, Lesley had jumped.

Sarah turned on her bike, slipped the helmet over her head, and pulled away from her spot in traffic. She steered the bike between the parked cars on the two-lane eastbound side of the bridge, drivers honking at her until she got to the roadblock. A police officer walked up, signaling her to halt.

She stopped the bike and leaned it on the kickstand. The officer spoke before she had a chance to get her helmet off. She ignored him and started for the walkway to take her down to the beach where the RCMP was bringing Lesley to shore. She only got two steps before the officer placed a hand on the inside of her elbow.

She stopped and looked down at his hand. Whatever expression was on her face made the officer release her arm, but he stayed close, crowding her.

"I was talking to you," the officer said. "Where do you think you're going? This area is blocked off. Can't you see there's a rescue underway?"

The cop was slightly overweight, sported a thin mustache, and mustard stains on his uniform.

Sarah pointed to the long line of traffic backed up along the bridge. The cars in the front of the line were close enough to listen in to their conversation. "That's a long line of stopped traffic—"

"I know what it is. Now get back on your bike and wait your turn like everyone else." He gestured at the bike. "Let's go."

In the water below, a small police boat floated near a uniformed officer swimming as he held the jumper's head above water. The drop couldn't be more than a hundred feet. The odds of the woman dying from that height were low.

This was a cry for help, and it had to do with her brother. Based on Vivian's notes, Sarah knew she would meet Greg Wright, Lesley's brother, soon enough.

"As I was saying." Sarah turned her attention back to the officer, who was losing his patience. He had pulled his radio out and held it close to his mouth. "I was parked twenty cars back in this line of traffic. I saw the girl. Before she jumped, I realized who she was."

"Great, now go back there and wait." He waved at the cars behind him. "Or I will place you in my cruiser until this is over. This area is blocked off for a reason." He shouted over his shoulder without taking his eyes off her. "Hey, Paulson, I might need you over here."

Sarah stepped closer, crowding him. "You're not listening. I know the jumper. Her name is Lesley Wright. Her brother's name is Greg Wright. I know the family, and I know why she jumped." Even though Sarah's sister, Vivian, hadn't supplied all the details, it was Sarah's job to work it out so that she got close to the cop rescuing the girl. His name was Barry Ashford, and she had a message for him. "When they pull her out, and she's inconsolable," she pointed over the side of the bridge at the RCMP boat as they hoisted Lesley out of the lake, "it will be of immense help if someone familiar is there to be with her. As a family friend, I will walk down to the beach and hold Lesley as she works through this horrific ordeal. From up here, all I can see are male officers. Imagine how humiliated and embarrassed she is, especially considering what she just did. Are you clear with what I'm trying to do now?"

The other cop, Paulson, must've not heard his colleague as he hadn't moved from his side of the traffic twenty feet away.

"Wow, what a mouth on such a little thing." He glanced over his shoulder at his partner. "Talking back to an officer of the law."

Sarah wanted to smack the stupid smirk off the cop's face but restrained herself.

"What if I say no?" he asked. "Would you get back in line, call her tonight at the psych ward?"

He was going to let her go down to the beach, but he wanted to have the power. He needed to make sure she knew that. She could go easy, play nice, and allow him to think that it was his decision, but that wouldn't be any fun.

She pointed at the news van parked at the side of the road. "If you try to stop me from walking down to the beach to console my dear friend, I will scream and shout and make a huge scene. I will yell Lesley's name loud enough for her to hear it. That Castanet news van will video you restraining me, and I will interview with them later, naming you as the one boy-in-blue who refused to allow that poor woman coming out of the water a dear friend in her time of need. So the question isn't whether I go to be with my friend. Rather, the question is whether you want your name in the news in a not-so-flattering way." She shrugged and spread her hands. "What'll it be? Am I free to go and be with my scared friend in this otherwise public area, or will you restrain me?"

The cop glanced at his partner for support. He was talking to the driver of a large blue pickup truck. Now that the girl had jumped, people wanted to get moving. This area would clear soon, and the police cruisers would be moved out of the way. In minutes, this spot would be public property again, without the roadblock.

The officer in front of her flexed his jaws, his lips thinned to a line, and his face tightened.

What's wrong with this guy?

"Get out of my sight," the cop said. "Go down there if you want. See if I care. They probably won't let you near that girl anyway, but that's not my problem."

He muttered, "Bitch," as he turned away.

She breathed deeply to calm herself. She couldn't let the cops, the street gang in blue, get under her skin so easily. Having left her family behind in Santa Rosa and Aaron back in Toronto, she was alone, sad, and hurt for almost killing Parkman in the vineyard behind her parents' house recently. She had notes from Vivian, things to do and stay busy with, but she had to learn how to tune out the officers with large egos and dangerous attitudes.

The boat carrying Lesley came ashore as Sarah scrambled down a small pile of rocks to the sandy beach. Another officer on the beach saw her and raised a hand.

"Excuse me, Miss. This area is blocked off for the time being."

Men held the boat steady in the shallow water while others helped Lesley out. One of the men held a large blanket.

"I'm Lesley's friend. That cop up there," she pointed to the road where she had just walked down from, "said I should come and talk to her, console her."

He waved. "Come along then."

Lesley was walking on her own, the blanket wrapped around her shoulders. Even though it was a hot August afternoon, she was soaked and shivering.

They steered her toward an ambulance parked on the

sand, rear doors open. Two paramedics walked toward Lesley and the officers who surrounded her.

Sarah started across the sand to rendezvous with them at the ambulance. Inside the police cordon, no one tried to stop her.

From a dozen feet away, Sarah got her first glimpse of Barry Ashford, the RCMP officer Vivian told her to antagonize. He was her real target. She didn't know why Vivian wanted her to do it but was sure she would learn soon enough.

Three male officers surrounded Lesley as she sat on the back of the ambulance. The female paramedic began to check her over.

"Excuse me," Sarah said as she edged in closer. "I'm with Lesley."

The officers turned toward her. Barry met her eyes. Sometimes a man's eyes told her a lot about the man. Some were calm, others scary. She'd seen smiling eyes, romantic eyes, and dark eyes. But Barry's eyes were dead. There was nothing there like she was looking at a rock or a chunk of black rubber.

She had also learned that when a man stared at her without blinking for more than five seconds, he either wanted to kill her or have sex with her, and Barry's body language didn't give away anything amorous.

"Who are you?" a cop to her right asked.

"Lesley's friend." She unlocked her eyes from Barry's. "She just went through something traumatic, and now she's surrounded by men. Clear out. Give her some space. I just spoke to her brother, Greg, and he wants me to be with her." Sarah edged between the officers, getting closer. "Come on, guys, give us some room. And you," she turned to Barry, "grab a towel and dry off closer to that Castanet News van. They're going to want your picture."

Without waiting for their reply, Sarah sat beside Lesley on the back of the ambulance. Recently she'd been inside a modified ambulance with a gunshot wound to the head. But that had healed well, and her long hair concealed the wound nicely.

"Greg sent you?" Lesley asked in a weak voice.

Lesley was high on something. It was written all over her face. High enough that her ordeal hadn't sobered her up.

"How are you feeling?" Sarah asked. "You okay now?"

The paramedic was checking something in Lesley's mouth. When they were done here, Lesley would probably be taken to the hospital, where they'd probably perform a psychological evaluation.

What Sarah had set out to do was done. She had needed to meet Lesley Wright and Barry Ashford, the man she would antagonize over the coming days.

"Listen, Lesley, I'm going to leave now. I will talk to your brother and tell him you're okay. Everything will work out. Just get dried up, deal with the authorities, and go home."

When their eyes met, Sarah saw Lesley's pain, her torment. Something bothered this girl deeply. Whatever it was, it was enough to kill herself.

"It'll be okay," Sarah said in a soft voice. "We'll work it out."

"You can't work it out," she whispered, then snuck a glance at Ashford, who had pulled her from the lake.

"Why are you looking at him?" Sarah asked.

"Because this is all his fault."

If Sarah hadn't been watching Lesley as she talked, she might've missed the slight twitch in Lesley's eyes, recognition that she'd said too much.

"Don't worry about that cop," Sarah said, matching Lesley's whisper.

Lesley snapped her head sideways. "You know? Greg told you?"

Sarah had no idea what Lesley was talking about but didn't want to lose her trust.

"Let's just say I know more than most. When can we talk again? I have an idea that soon all your troubles will disappear. Forever."

Lesley lit up. She leaned closer and lowered her voice even more. "How?"

Sarah shook her head. "When we meet. Not here."

"Okay, Twisted Tomato on Bernard Avenue, downtown. Meet me there tomorrow at six in the evening. We'll have a coffee and maybe some food. Then you can tell me everything."

"Deal." Sarah stuck out her hand, and Lesley shook it. When she glanced at Barry, he was watching them. Whatever he was doing to this girl would stop, or Sarah would make it stop even more so because he was a cop. It seemed everywhere she went, the more things she had to deal with; it almost always led back to the street gang in blue, and that was really starting to get on her nerves.

"Tomorrow night, then." Sarah rose from the back of the ambulance. She started for the pathway that led back to the road where her bike was parked. Just before she reached the rocks where she had to climb, Barry's voice stopped her.

"Who are you?" he asked in a deadpan voice.

Sarah waited a moment with her back to him, then turned around. His hair was drying and tousled from a towel. His uniform had mostly dried and wasn't pasted to his skin. Everyone would call him a hero for pulling Lesley out of the water, but he was involved in something criminal. Vivian felt the only way to figure that something out was to anger him.

"Who wants to know?" she asked, her stare and emotionless voice as cold as his.

"Why were you talking to that girl?"

"And this is your business? How?"

He stepped closer. "She jumped from that bridge. She tried to kill herself." His voice rose a notch. "When we pulled her out of the water, she was weak and vulnerable. So I want to know who you are. What credentials do you have that allow you to comfort someone in her current mental state?"

'And you're qualified to assess her mental state?" Sarah stood her ground. "You are a police officer. You had a job to do. You did it. Whoopee. Congratulations. Woman saved." She stepped so close she could smell his stale breath. "But that's it. That's as far as it goes. Tell me, where is it written that a cop can assess her mental state? Where's your doctorate? Where is it legislated that you're suddenly her guardian?" Sarah looked him up and down. "Your ego is too big. Do you think because you pulled her out of the water that that's it? You get to pick who she talks to? Boy, what do they teach you at cop school?" She turned away and started up the hill, but he grabbed her arm.

"We're not finished here," he said, his tone serious. Something she had said had gotten under his skin.

"Release. My. Arm." She snuck a glance at the news van. The cameraman was aiming a camera at them. "You are being broadcast live on Castanet. If you test me, I will make a scene, and your hero moment will diffuse in a second."

The hand came away.

She stepped up the rocks and turned back to him, looking down. Two other cops were crossing the sand to see what was going on.

"We'll meet again, Officer Ashford."

At the mention of his name, his eyes widened. He tried to hide it, but the effort was wasted.

"And when we do, you won't be too happy."

"Are you threatening me?"

"Let's just say I know what you did and what you've been up to." Vivian hadn't revealed that part yet, but it felt right as she spoke the lie. Whatever he was up to, letting him know she was onto it would add an element of paranoia.

The other officers now stood beside him.

"Everything okay here, Ashford?" the one on the left said.

"Yes, I was just escorting this woman back to her vehicle across the beach."

Sarah started up the grassy embankment. A minute later, she looked back at Ashford before reaching for her bike. He stood alone on the sand and watched her.

But this time, his face seemed darker, angrier. It matched the dead look in his eyes.

His hand rested on the holster on his belt.

It was a subtle threat, but it was a threat.

Sarah knew that she had accomplished what she came here to do.

In the coming days, it would be easy to rankle him. She looked forward to meeting him again.

Next time she wouldn't be so nice.

Chapter 2

KELOWNA, BRITISH COLUMBIA, WAS a well-developed, pretty city. It sat in the Okanagan Valley on Okanagan Lake, with the Canadian Rockies Mountain range surrounding it. Sarah had read up on Kelowna and found out it was ranked the eighth happiest city in Canada. It was also ranked number one for having the highest crime rate of any city in Canada per capita.

Sarah steered her motorcycle up Bernard Avenue, through downtown Kelowna, past small shops and the tourists walking the streets during the height of summer. At any other time in her life, she would love to rent a room for a few days with Aaron, swim in the lake, and take in some of the nightlife.

But that wouldn't happen because Aaron was in Toronto, and Sarah was here, in Kelowna, doing what she did best. She missed him. His touch, his tender soul. But she had to pursue her calling, do what the messages from her dead sister asked, and keep doing it indefinitely.

Did she deserve Aaron? Did she deserve friends after what she did to Parkman? They had told her that she was beating herself up over a mistake, but what they failed to see was that this mistake almost cost Parkman, her loyal friend, his life. Sarah never bluffed. When she pulled out her weapon and aimed it at someone, she intended to use it. Having aimed the weapon at Parkman with intent meant he was about to be shot. The only reason she hesitated as long as she did, which was out of character for her, was because it was Parkman. In her mind, he hadn't hesitated when it came to shooting her, and she didn't want to be as filthy or as cruel.

But it was that hesitation that saved his life. Seconds before she would have shot him, she discovered he wasn't at fault. He hadn't been the one who shot her in the head as her choppy memory had led her to believe.

To have her friend's death that close and on her conscience was too much to bear. She wasn't beating herself up over it. She was ashamed, disgusted with herself, and unwilling to accept his love or friendship. She didn't feel worthy.

Maybe one day that'll change, but for now, it is what it is.

Sarah turned right at the Ellis Street intersection and headed toward Highway 97. Before leaving Santa Rosa, California, with Vivian's messages clear in her mind, Sarah had contacted a couple who were renting a furnished home in McKinley Landing, a quiet suburb on the north end of the city. Highway 97 would take her to Glenmore Road, which led to McKinley Landing, where she had an appointment to meet the landlords.

It was funny how the bridge was named William Bennett Bridge, and she was to rent a house on Bennett Road. Bennett had been the name of the first girl she ever saved from a kidnapping all those years ago. A relative of Mary Bennett's saved Sarah's life in a crypt in Esztergom, Hungary, a few years back. Maybe this was a sign that her life was about to go back to the way it was. Maybe Sarah could be redeemed.

She made it on time for her appointment on Bennett Road. The wooded area was quiet and exactly what Sarah wanted and needed.

She parked behind the minivan in the driveway. Birds flitted in the tall pine trees above, a breeze rustled the branches, and the sun fell behind the mountains over Okanagan Lake in a stunning view. It couldn't be nicer, but something inside Sarah shouted that she didn't deserve this relaxed setting. This was too pretty, too serene.

Why, Vivian? Why this house? Why not some dirty basement apartment in the city?

"Sarah Roberts?"

She placed her helmet on the seat of her bike. When she turned toward the house, a woman wearing a long red dress stood on the front porch, a broom in her hand. Sarah remembered her name was Joan. Dressing like she was heading out for an evening of dancing while holding a broom made Sarah smile. It was the first genuine smile since she left Santa Rosa, and it didn't last long.

"I was just cleaning up the porch. We haven't been here in a while." The woman gestured at the tall trees in the large front yard. "We get a lot of pine needles and cones covering the grass and front walkway every year. They really start to fall in October and November, so it's not so bad yet." She leaned the broom against the wall beside the door. "Come on in. I've got iced tea ready. We'll take a tour of the house."

Sarah waited a moment, her hand resting on the dome of her helmet. Whether she deserved this or not or was willing to allow any pleasures in her life, it was what Vivian wanted. There had to be a reason, and it probably had nothing to do with Sarah being comfortable, so on those terms, she moved forward up the driveway.

The house to her left sat at the end of the road. It pied out, giving extra room to the yard. The dwelling to the right was closer to the house she wanted to rent. There was movement in the front window.

Someone was watching her.

She made to enter the house as if she hadn't seen a thing, waited a moment, and jumped back.

A woman, who looked to be in her sixties, stared out at Sarah's bike from the corner window of the neighbor's house. The woman wore black pants and a black top.

Maybe while I'm here, I'll be the subject of conversation for all the neighbors.

She entered the house, closed the door behind her, and turned into the kitchen. Joan leaned against the island in the center of the large chef's kitchen. A man stood by the fridge.

"Sarah, I'd like you to meet my husband."

Sarah shook his hand. He had a firm grip for a man in his seventies.

Did only old people buy houses out in the boonies?

"Mike, right?" she asked.

He nodded.

"And Joan? Names can be difficult for me, but I didn't forget from our phone call. Terrible thing what happened to your previous tenants."

"Yes," Joan said. "When you and I talked on the phone, I was still pretty upset."

"I seem to forget what you said about them. Did they just up and leave?"

"We think so." Joan looked at Mike. He leaned on the silver fridge door and nodded for her to continue. "We have a house in Costa Rica." She grabbed a tall glass and poured iced tea as she talked. "Every year, we head down there in the winter and return in the summer. Only in the last two winters have we rented out our home." She passed the glass along the island counter to Sarah. "It helps as we're retired now. But it's been getting harder and harder to find suitable tenants who are willing to stay only six or seven months." She glanced out the huge bay window in the living room at the setting sun as it colored the sky a deep red above the lake. "Come on out on the balcony. We can talk there."

Once on the balcony, Joan started up again.

"This was the first year we thought we'd stay in Costa Rica for the summer and rent this house for the entire year. Last month, when rent was due for July, nothing showed up in our account. Then nothing for August, either. We called up to the house and got no answer. I had Deborah from next door come over to see if everything was all right." Joan looked down at her half-full glass of iced tea. "Our tenants had left, and some of our precious glasses and china left with them. A few paintings as well." She met Sarah's eyes. "So Mike and I flew back, and here we are, looking for a new tenant."

"Did they leave a note?" Sarah asked. "Did you have any indication that they were going to split on you? Any signs?" She sipped her drink. Canadians always put too much sugar in their iced tea. She tried to control the grimace by turning it into an awkward smile.

"We knew Jacob worked at the Orchard Park Mall here in Kelowna. He was a retail manager. When we went to the store in the mall, the employees said he just didn't show up for work one day. Mind you, we don't normally drive around trying to find our tenants, it's just, he signed a lease. The money is due. Or was due since we're hoping you'll take the house. I wanted my stuff back, too." She sipped her tea again. "Our return trip to Costa Rica is booked, and I'm afraid we're out of time." She raised a hand to block the setting sun from her eyes. "I'm sorry. I shouldn't be trying to get you to sign the dotted line when we haven't even shown you around yet."

Joan took Sarah on a tour while Mike sat in the living room and read a Clive Barker novel. They took a half hour, covering all the appliances, where the fuse box was, and how to operate the underground sprinkler system.

"Are you sure it's not too big for one person?" Joan asked.

Sarah shook her head. "I need the peace and quiet."

Something caught Joan's eye. She pointed at the area where the bullet had entered Sarah's head months ago.

"What happened there?" Joan asked. "Looks like you have some hair missing."

"Dumb accident on the bike." She hated lying but telling her potential landlords the truth would only scare them. "They shaved the hair around the area to give me stitches."

She waved it off. "It's nothing, really." To change the subject, she said, "So you want a damage deposit and first month's rent."

"That'll be all we need." She handed a booklet over. "The phone, the cable, and the internet stay in our name. All you do is maintain the bills until we return. Everything else is in this book. Emergency call numbers and bank deposit slips with our account number for the monthly rent."

"Perfect."

Sarah got the money order out that she had prepared for their meeting and handed it over. Previously, they had emailed the lease. This meeting had been necessary but was only a formality.

"You'll love it here," Joan said. "Peaceful, quiet, a great place to get all your writing done."

Sarah had told them on the phone that she was writing a series of books. She was on her fourth and needed a writer's retreat like their home to finish writing in a serene setting.

"This will work out perfectly," Sarah said.

"Mike," Joan called. "We're done here. Let's head back to the hotel."

Outside the front door, Joan pointed at the house on the pied-out end of the street. "That's the Rankins's house. They head to Arizona in two months for the winter. We haven't seen them since we've been here, but they're usually around all summer." She turned to the house where the nosy neighbor had watched her bike from the window. "Over there, you have Deborah and her husband—"

A woman stepped from the bushes, a tray of cookies in her hands. It was the neighbor who had been watching from the window.

"Speak of the devil," Joan said. "Here's Debbie now. Come on over and meet your new neighbor."

Mike exited the house and shut the front door. He headed for their rental car as Joan and Sarah walked up to meet Debbie. Why didn't Mike want to join them? Maybe bad blood. But how? Why? Wasn't Deborah a help when they needed her? Didn't she come and check on the previous tenants?

"Debbie, I'd like you to meet Sarah Roberts, our new tenant."

"How do you do?" Debbie asked.

They shook hands. Debbie was younger than Sarah had thought and stronger. Having only seen her from a short distance and through a window, Debbie appeared older, but she was in her forties or maybe late forties. She had an intensity to her that Sarah couldn't understand. It was like she was dangerous. Her eyes glared when she talked like she was ready to hurt someone. It didn't fit with her smile and the way she carried herself. Everyone had a secret, a uniqueness about them. With people like Debbie, the secret was scary. The kind of thing people didn't want to hear, and no one talked about it unless they were at their therapist's office. Or in a courtroom.

"You're renting the Smith's place?" Debbie asked.

Sarah nodded. "Yes, I am."

"Terrible thing what happened to the previous tenants."

What did that mean? Didn't they just leave?

From what Joan said, they had simply vacated the property and left no forwarding address. They did a midnight run after stealing some of her possessions. Unless Debbie knew more than Joan did. Maybe that was Debbie's secret.

She watched the street. She watched the comings and goings of her neighbors. She probably saw some of what happened to the previous tenants.

"I thought they just up and left," Sarah said.

"Yes." Debbie looked away. Her eyes stopped on Mike sitting in the car. She turned back to Sarah. "One day, they were here; the next, they were gone."

"They?"

"Jacob and his girlfriend. I have my suspicions, though."

Joan cut in. "But Debbie, nothing in the house ever indicated …"

"I know, I know." She raised a hand, the other still holding the tray of cookies. "It's just, while you were in Costa Rica, I saw the kind of people coming and going." She glanced at Sarah. "Do you do drugs?"

"Deborah!" Joan gasped.

"It's okay, Joan," Sarah said. "I don't take anything. Never have. Why do you ask?"

"Because I think Jacob and his girlfriend were on heroin. Selling it or using it."

"Really? Heroin? Why that specific drug?"

"It's what killed them."

"Now, Debbie," Joan cut in again. "We don't know if they're dead. They just moved out to who knows where."

"That sounds like dead to me."

"Did you get the Rankins' back door fixed yet?" Joan asked.

"What happened to their back door?" Sarah asked.

"When Jacob and his girlfriend were living here, they broke in next door." Debbie gestured with a nod of her head at the last house on the street. "I check on the house periodically and saw the back sliding door was off its track, and the lock had been picked. It still locks, but with a little pressure, it can be dislodged."

"Is it fixed?" Joan asked.

"No one comes down here, Joan. It's a dead-end street and a quiet neighborhood. Now that Jacob is gone, there's no concern. The door still locks."

Debbie's eyes revealed questionable sanity to Sarah. The only secret about her was probably that she was slightly nuts.

"Are those peanut butter cookies?" Sarah asked, wanting to change the subject. It was odd Deborah couldn't see that talking about the previous tenants bothered Joan.

"Yes, I brought them for you. A welcome-to-the-neighborhood present."

"That's very kind. Thank you."

"Well, we must be going," Joan said. "If you need anything, Debbie and her husband stay here all winter. Her husband works in Kelowna."

Debbie handed the tray to Sarah.

"The keys are on the kitchen counter," Joan added. "Everything is set up, so all you need to do is unpack your clothes and get groceries."

"Thank you. I'm sure everything will be fine."

Joan walked away, got in the car with Mike, and they pulled out of the driveway. Sarah was alone with Debbie as the area darkened further, the sun gone behind the mountains now.

"I guess we'll see each other again," Sarah said.

She wanted to grab her laptop off the bike and hook up to the internet. She had work to do, and she needed to place a call to a local cleaning company. According to Vivian, Sarah was to hire a maid to come to the house weekly, whether she needed it or not.

"We should have you over for coffee or tea one evening when my husband's here. I'm sure he'd love to meet you."

"That would be great," Sarah said as she backed away.

"If you need anything, just call. Our number is in that booklet Joan gave you. Also, if you think someone's prowling the area or up to no good, call us first."

What could the neighbors do when the police are trained to handle those kinds of situations? Although I wouldn't call the police.

"Shouldn't I call the police first?" Sarah asked.

"Didn't Joan tell you?"

Sarah shook her head.

"My husband is an RCMP officer for the city of Kelowna. Barry takes his job seriously, especially in the community where he lives. That's why we knew the previous tenants were into heroin. Barry recognized some of the dealers visiting Joan's house before the previous tenants disappeared. But you needn't worry about that anymore. As soon as Jacob left, the drug traffic to your front door stopped." She backed up a few more steps. "I didn't want to go into detail in front of Joan. It upsets her to think she made such a bad choice with her last renter. I'm sure you're a much better fit." Debbie turned away and started for the bushes that separated their yards.

So that was why Vivian wanted her to rent this house, a much larger place than she needed.

Because Deborah and Barry Ashford were her neighbors.

The man she was supposed to antagonize lived right next door.

How deliciously malicious of you, Vivian.

Sarah entered her new home, slammed the door, and grabbed the cordless phone.

Time to hire a cleaning company.

Chapter 3

Barry unlocked the front door of his house quietly. None of the lights were on, which indicated his wife had already gone to bed.

Or she's passed out from too much booze.

He set his briefcase on the foyer table, hooked his keys into their holder on the wall, and started for the laundry basket in the bathroom. Deb would have to do a load in the morning. As soon as his uniform was in the laundry basket, he went back to the kitchen, pulled one of the new wine glasses from the cabinet, and poured a glass of red wine.

After the interviews, the paperwork he had to fill out regarding the jumper at the bridge, and the endless questions from the press, he was exhausted and looked forward to sleep. But that girl from the beach, the pretty one who talked to Lesley Wright at the ambulance, had stayed on his mind the whole time.

She had said, "Let's just say I know what you did, and I know what you've been up to."

What could she have meant? Barry had never seen her before. He didn't even get her name. No one at the beach knew who she was; even Lesley admitted to having just met her. But Lesley added that the strange girl knew Greg, Lesley's brother.

He took his wine and walked out to the deck to sit under the stars. He needed to relax, clear his head, and figure out what to do about the girl. Maybe she was someone's sister looking for revenge for one of the girls Barry had flash-blooded with. He loved his flash-blooding games and couldn't imagine stopping them. Not even for the strange girl at the beach.

He slid the door closed quietly and walked to the railing.

"You're home late."

He jumped, nearly dropping his glass over the edge of the deck's railing.

"Deb, what are you doing?"

"The same thing you are. Sipping wine on the deck under that beautiful moon. But tell me something. Why is it just because I'm doing it, there's suspicion involved?"

"I wasn't questioning where you go or what you drink. I was merely asking why you were trying to scare me." He steadied himself with another sip of wine and looked away. The moon's reflection glimmered across the surface of the lake.

"I won't argue that sitting on my deck at one in the morning as I relax before bed could be construed as having devious intent on my part. Maybe I've lived with a cop too long. Why is everything about motive with you? Ulterior or otherwise?"

"Look, Deb, I don't want to fight tonight."

"Neither do I."

She grunted, then swallowed a couple of times. She was probably just as drunk as she was on other nights when he worked afternoons. It'd been the same old thing, over and over. Unhappy, disgruntled, idle, and drinking. He had no idea what else she did with her day, but he knew one thing: whatever it was, it wasn't productive.

"Answer me something," she said.

"Hmm."

"Why did you save that girl on the bridge today?"

"News travels fast."

"It was on Castanet."

He turned to face her silhouette. "You expect me to not act when I'm at work. I have a job to do, an image to upkeep."

"What will that bitch Lesley say to the police? What will show up in her statement?"

"I was there for that. I can assure you, she'll say nothing that'll incriminate us."

"Oh, you can assure me, all right." Then under her breath, "Bullshit."

"Look, not tonight." He took a large gulp of his wine. "I need to relax. Tomorrow I'll figure everything out. I'll talk to Greg and find out what happened. Once I get to the bottom of it, we'll smooth everything over. It's called damage control. Nothing can go wrong. Besides, I'm the one who dove in and saved her. No one would believe a word out of her mouth if she started taking shots at me. So just relax. Stay calm. Losing our cool could screw things up. I'll handle everything."

"That's what I'm afraid of," she said, barely above a whisper.

She was trying to ignite him. He had to resist her bait. Otherwise, the neighbors would hear this fight. In his mood, restraint would be difficult.

He tossed the rest of his wine over the railing and started for the door.

"I'm leaving," she said.

He stopped, a firm grip on the handle.

"What?"

She waited a full five seconds, then said, "I'm leaving."

"Leaving? For what, a vacation? Or leaving for good?"

"For good. There's too much heat. We've gone too far. We have to go together, or I'm leaving alone."

He let go of the handle and faced her. "Where will you go? Your sister's place? We can't afford that."

How could she leave him at such a critical time in their marriage? Everything they had done was a joint effort. They were the originators of flash-blooding in Kelowna and were doing it well. Their small group kept it tight-knit. Not much was known about flash-blooding, but Barry was an expert at sharing drug-infused blood, and his group fed off him as if he were a vampire and only his blood sustained them. His price was minimal, and most of the time, the girls didn't mind. If any of them ratted him out, he could spend a lot of time in jail, but it was too late to worry about that. He was in too far, and so were his fellow flash-blooders.

A few people had caused them trouble in the past, but he had dealt with it. They either quit, and he never saw them again, or they took off for another city. As long as the members enjoyed themselves, his risk was minimal. Lesley's stupid suicide attempt could be trouble. Maybe she should have died, but he was the closest officer to her. He couldn't *not* jump in and pull her from the water in front of his colleagues.

Then there was that girl at the beach. The one who knows what he's been up to. She could prove to be a problem. There was something about her brazenness.

"I don't care about money," Deb said. "I don't care about anything anymore." She threw her glass against the railing, where it shattered and dropped silently to the grass below. "You call this a marriage? A marriage of what? Two fools destined to die of an overdose or end up in jail?"

"Keep your voice down. Come inside. We'll talk there."

He slid the door to the end of the track and stepped inside. She couldn't leave. She knew too much. She could ruin everything. Flash-blooding had become his thing, his fun time. He couldn't stop. He wouldn't stop. Not for her. Not for anybody.

If she packed a bag, he would have to prevent her from leaving at all costs. Maybe she could be tied up in the basement for a while. He could feed her and offer a bucket for a toilet. That would teach her to obey better.

He would hate to have to do that, but he would make an exception for his wife.

Some women could be taught manners, but others had to be forced.

Forcing his wife to learn would be a pleasure.

Chapter 4

THE MID-MORNING SUN woke Sarah in her new bed. Yesterday had been a long day on the road during her drive to Kelowna. She rolled over to enjoy the warmth and comfort.

She had an hour until her appointment. The cleaning company had scheduled someone to pop in to assess the size of the house and what she wanted to be done so they could offer a quote. The house's interior was spotless, but an appointment for next week for the first cleaning would work out well

After the free cleaning estimate today, there wasn't much left to do, as per Vivian's notes. Sarah still planned to meet with Lesley Wright at the Twisted Tomato downtown Kelowna that evening. And she still planned on antagonizing Barry Ashford, her next-door neighbor, but that was it.

She sat up in bed, rubbed her eyes, and stared out at the lake. The view from the bedroom was spectacular. She could get used to this life. Nice, expensive house. Million-dollar views. Cleaning lady.

She flopped back in bed. The only sad part was Aaron wasn't here to enjoy it with her. They could cook breakfast in their robes. Eat on the deck overlooking the lake. Have wine with lunch, take a nap after sex, and then watch movies into the evening, cuddling. She had enough money from when her parents sold their old house before moving to Santa Rosa and new money from Oliver Payne. It was his daughter who had shot Sarah in the head. Oliver was rich and paid a lot of people off for their pain and suffering.

This wasn't a vacation, though. Vivian wasn't sending out her usual messages, but this was still important; she just didn't know how.

Her hand numbed. It worked up her arm.

"Okay, okay …"

Sarah grabbed the pad and pen beside the bed and lay down. Her eyes rolled back in her head. A moment later, she snapped awake to a new message.

She read what her sister wanted her to do.

"Why do I need duct tape, handcuffs, and bear spray?" she asked out loud. "Am I going hunting?"

The clock ticked audibly.

"Shit, he'll be here in just over half an hour."

She set the pen down, left the pad on the bed, and headed for the shower. Twenty-five minutes later, she looked out the front window in time to see a small Kia pull in with a sticker on the driver's side door that said, ReadyMaid House Cleaning Service. The driver parked behind her BMW bike and got out.

She unlocked the front door and waited on the porch. Her

skin immediately grew damp with sweat in the summer swelter. Mosquitoes buzzed around her head, and a fly entered the house through the open door behind her.

"You're on time," she said as the man walked up the driveway.

Small and slightly unsure of himself, a geeky-looking guy, his legs long and gangly, strode up quickly, fumbling and almost dropping the pad secured in his arm.

"Hi, my name's Derek. I'm from ReadyMaid, here to do an estimate on the house."

His voice was too high for a man in his twenties.

"I'm Sarah. I'm the one who called."

"Great. Can you walk me through the house and tell me what you want to be cleaned on a weekly basis?"

"Sure, come on in."

As she showed him around the house, Sarah studied Derek, watching for anything weird or out of place, wondering why Vivian told her to call this company. She never took her eyes off him or turned her back to him. He seemed harmless, but until she discovered why Vivian directed her to this company, he was her suspect.

"You live here alone?" he asked when they returned to the kitchen.

"How does that matter?"

"Oh. I'm sorry," he said in his weak, giggly voice. "I was just wondering why you would want to have the house cleaned weekly if it's only going to be you living here. The norm with our company is monthly or bi-weekly if a larger number of people live in the house, like a family."

He seemed quite nervous, like he wasn't used to being around girls much.

"Will it be men or women who clean the house?" Sarah asked.

"Only women. I just do the estimates."

He was around women all the time if ReadyMaid only had female employees.

"To answer your other question, I'm a little anal about cleanliness. My house has to be clean at all times, and I don't want to be the one doing it. Once a week is a good schedule for me."

"Are there more rooms down that hall?" he asked.

Sarah walked toward the bedroom and en suite, waving for him to follow. As he examined the house, he scribbled notes on his notepad.

"So that's three bedrooms, two bathrooms, the living room and dining room, and the kitchen. Sound about right?" he asked.

They were in the master bedroom; the curtains still pulled back to reveal the stunning view. Derek stopped to stare.

"Wow, very pretty from here," he said.

"It is." *But you're not here for the view.*

He glanced down at the pad Sarah had left on the bed earlier.

Vivian's list was clear and in big letters.

Handcuffs, duct tape, bear spray ...

His eyes widened as he read the note.

She put a hand on his shoulder and physically turned him away from the pad. "Hey, pal, let's go to the kitchen. We can finish up there."

"Yes, yes, okay."

More nervous now, less assured, he stumbled back to the

kitchen, almost dropping his pad twice.

What's this all about, Vivian? What am I doing here?

He set the pad down at the island in the center of the kitchen and checked a few things off.

"A couple more questions, and I'll be on my way," he said.

"Shoot."

"What day of the week would you want the cleaner to come?"

"Tuesdays."

"Morning or afternoon?"

"Morning."

"Will you be paying by cash or credit card?"

"Cash."

"When you give the cleaner the money, she'll give you a receipt.'

Sarah nodded.

He wrote something on his pad.

"Will you be home when the cleaner comes?" He kept his eyes averted like he was afraid she would see something in them if he met her gaze. "If not, will you leave a hidden key for us to enter? Our girls are all bonded. And is the house alarmed? If so, we would need the code."

Is that normal? Do strangers allow others to enter their houses with a key and an alarm code?

"No access whatsoever," Sarah said. "Only when I'm here to unlock the door myself."

"That's fine. We have to ask because some people give us a key and then forget about the alarm, and boom, we set it off." He ran a finger down his pad again. When it stopped, he said, "Any pets? Dogs or cats?"

"None."

Maybe Vivian wants Sarah to give these guys unfettered access to the house.

"Listen, Derek, change my answer on the key. I will leave one under the flower pot by the front door. There's no alarm on the house. All I ask is they knock first. If there's no answer, they can let themselves in."

He scratched something out and then added a new note.

"Perfect. Well, I guess that wraps it up. I'll check the schedule and get back to you to confirm the first appointment and give you the price quote from my notes here." He collected his pad and started for the front door, still not looking at her as if he was embarrassed. "After the first cleaning, we'll call to see how satisfied you are and schedule the next one. How does that sound?"

"Perfect."

She waited until his shoes were on and he had stepped out the door.

"Hey, Derek?"

He stopped on the front steps and turned around, meeting her eyes.

"Yes?"

"What went through your mind when you read that note on my bed?"

He stumbled, his eyes widened, and his lips tightened. The tips of his white teeth showed through his thin lips for a moment. He was embarrassed and genuinely so. If Vivian meant for her to meet this guy because he was doing something illegal, she probably had the wrong guy. Derek was so nervous and bashful that he looked ready to piss his pants.

"Uh, I'm sorry. I'm not sure what it said. I just looked down, but I'm, please forgive me …" he said, stumbling over his words.

"It's okay. Just tell me your boss's name. Who owns ReadyMaid in case I want to lodge a complaint?"

"Um, the Wrights own ReadyMaid. Greg and his sister, Lesley Wright. She's usually the one who does the estimates, but they sent me because Lesley called in sick today."

"I'm sure she did. Goodbye, Derek."

Sarah shut the door and leaned against the back of it.

"Holy shit, Vivian. You could've let me know. A simple note. Damn girl, what's with all the mystery?"

Sarah pushed off the door and went for her keys. She needed to explore Kelowna, pick up the items from Vivian's list, buy a few groceries, and then meet Lesley at the Twisted Tomato at six.

Lesley would have an interesting story about why she had to end her life, and Sarah intended to find everything out to see how it connected to Barry Ashford.

Something was wrong with ReadyMaid, and something was wrong with Lesley. And in a week, a representative of ReadyMaid was going to be in Sarah's house cleaning it.

She smacked her hands together.

"Maybe this is going to be a busy week after all."

Chapter 5

Spy vs. Spy, a store on Kirshner Street in Kelowna, had all the supplies Sarah needed. The GPS tracker she got had a two-week battery life, and the small black box she placed it in had strong magnets that would attach to RCMP officer Barry Ashford's cruiser and stay attached under almost any conditions.

She could stick it under his car, log into the tracker from her computer, and monitor wherever he drove within an accuracy of five feet. The tracker was also motion sensitive. When there wasn't any motion, it turned off, saving the battery. The best feature of the new units was that they logged breadcrumbs. If she hadn't watched his action for a day or two, the tracker logged where he went and how long he stayed at each spot. She could easily go back and view all the places he visited, how often and for how long, hopefully pinpointing whatever it was Vivian had sent her to find.

She strolled down Bernard Avenue, heading to the Twisted Tomato after walking along the beach. Kelowna was a summer city. The streets were crowded with families, teenagers here to party, and other tourists looking for a sunny place on the beach in a town surrounded by mountains. Kelowna was beautiful and wasn't just considered the eighth happiest city in Canada; it was also called the whitest city in Canada because of the high ratio of Caucasians living here.

But the statistic Sarah was most interested in was the one that ranked Kelowna as the number one city in all of Canada with the highest crime rate per capita. Something was wrong in paradise. Kelowna's drug problems, biker gangs, murders, and petty crimes were all found online for anyone to browse. There were websites devoted to stamping out crime in Kelowna. Recently, the City of Kelowna opened a John School where men who hired prostitutes could be educated on the mental and emotional damage they caused to the women they hired by the hour. Sometimes, the judge handling a solicitation charge in court would allow the charges to be dropped as long as the man graduated from John School.

In Sarah's research, she had located the massage parlors and the bawdy houses in Kelowna, which seemed to be doing a brisk business, unhindered by police interference.

Kelowna was a beautiful city, but on the surface, it looked like the authorities weren't doing enough to rid the city of its crime. She even suspected that police officers were contributing to the problem.

She stopped in front of the Twisted Tomato and scanned the street. People walked by, some laughed, and some wore the determined look of heading somewhere important. There was the sound of a horn a block over, an engine revved, and a woman's laughter. It all made her think of Aaron. He had called earlier, but she didn't take the call. She wasn't ready.

I wish you were here, and this was a vacation for the two of us.

She pulled on the door and stepped inside the restaurant. A batch of tables spread out evenly on her right. To the left, along the gold-painted wall, sat a long line of bright red—tomato red—booths. Most of the tables and booths were occupied, but a single booth sat empty near the back.

A young brunette in a black dress stepped up to Sarah.

"Just one?"

"No, I'm meeting someone in a few minutes. We'd prefer a booth."

"Great. There's one open down here. Follow me."

Once at the table, the woman left a menu and walked away. Sarah realized she hadn't eaten as soon as the smell from the kitchen hit her, and she picked up the menu.

The front door opened. Another couple. The brunette was telling them there would be a five-minute wait.

Two men sat at a table at least ten feet away. They had been watching her. Both men averted their eyes the instant she looked at them.

She lost focus on the menu in her hands. Why had they been watching her? Did Lesley send someone to check her out first? If so, what was Lesley into that made her so paranoid?

Sarah snuck a glance back at the men. They were chatting softly, ignoring her. One ate soup, the other a thick sandwich. It was the one with the soup that struck her as familiar in some way.

Where would I know him from?

She didn't have a gun. Crossing the American/Canadian border with a sidearm would have been reckless and stupid. The Army Surplus store in town could only offer her specialized knives or dog spray. It was the spray that worked on four-legged *and* two-legged animals. It seemed she encountered more two-legged animals than any other kind.

"Ready to order?" the waitress said.

Sarah jumped as she had been lost in her thoughts.

"Oh, I'm sorry," the waitress said as she offered a nervous giggle. "I didn't mean to scare you."

"It's okay. I was too focused on the menu."

"Are you ready, or would you like me to come back?"

"I'm waiting for someone else. When she's here, we'll order together."

"Great idea." The waitress walked away.

Sarah took the opportunity to check out the men again. The man with the soup was watching her and wasn't afraid that she knew it. He slurped his spoon, his eyes boring through her.

Then, like a plug entering a socket, she remembered where she recognized him.

He was one of the men who asked Barry Ashford if everything was okay yesterday on the beach when Barry was talking to Sarah.

What's he doing here? Coincidence or planned?

She straightened in her seat. It couldn't be a coincidence. She had to assume the man with the sandwich was also a cop and that they were armed.

She couldn't leave. What if Lesley showed up and she was gone? It wasn't illegal for two girls to meet and talk.

What could the cops possibly be doing here unless it was a coincidence?

Would Barry ask them to spy on Lesley? If so, what did Lesley have over Barry?

Probably what Vivian sent me to find out.

It was moments like this that she wished Vivian were clearer. Knowing her purpose in Kelowna could embolden her and give her the leverage she needed to keep the cops at bay. She didn't trust the police much anyway. They had to earn her trust like Parkman did all those years ago.

Going with the fact that they were here, exactly where she was supposed to meet Lesley, who was now a few minutes late, meant they were here for more than the tasty cuisine.

Sarah set the menu down, twisted in her seat, and started to stand.

A firm hand on her shoulder stopped her.

Barry Ashford looked down. "Not so fast." He cleared his throat. "It's a busy place." In a lower voice, he said, "Don't make a scene, or I'll arrest you, and we'll have this conversation downtown in private." He released her shoulder and waved a finger back and forth as if she were a naughty child. "And you don't want to talk to me in private. It won't bode well for you."

As he squeezed into the booth opposite her, she sized him up. Dressed in civilian clothes. He had a gun stashed in a shoulder holster hidden under a light brown summer jacket. He was probably packing an ankle holster as well, not to mention the guns the two men a table over were probably packing. Barry had placed his backup in the restaurant before the arranged meeting with Lesley. Sarah didn't know Barry well yet, but she wouldn't put it past him to beat it out of Lesley to learn about tonight's meeting with Sarah.

"Where's Lesley?" Sarah asked, keeping her tone level and emotionless.

"None of your concern." He grabbed a small container by the salt and pepper, slid it across the table, tapped it once, and pulled a toothpick out.

"Don't," Sarah said as images of Parkman assailed her.

He stopped.

"Don't what?"

"Drop the toothpick."

He looked down at it and laughed. "Why?"

"Set the toothpick down, or I walk out of here."

She would not talk to him with thoughts of Parkman on her mind.

Barry set the toothpick aside.

"Is that your way of gaining control? Are you showing me your prowess, your feminine strength?" He smiled, enjoying his own sarcastic voice. "Because from where I'm sitting, you look like a pretty little girl, not butchy and tough."

"Where's Lesley?"

"Straight to business. I like that." He glanced at his backup.

"Don't worry about them," she said. "They're well fed and ready if you need them. We're talking here. Pay the fuck attention to me. Never underestimate your enemy."

"Whoa." He raised his hands. "Take it easy, tough girl." He lowered his arms to the table and placed his palms flat. "You're in my town now, whoever you are, and I want to know why you're here."

The waitress stepped into view. "Hi, Barry," she said. "I saw you wave. You guys ready to order?"

His dead eyes never left Sarah. "I think we'll have two coffees to start. I'll motion for you when we need more."

"Nothing for me," Sarah said, her eyes not leaving Barry's.

Maneuvering himself into her booth when she was expecting Lesley only motivated her to raise her antagonizing to a new level. Very soon, Barry Ashford would grow to hate and despise Sarah Roberts.

"Then just one coffee, Melissa," Barry said. The waitress stepped away from the table. "You're being awfully mean."

"Last time I'll ask. Where's Lesley?"

"Okay, take it easy. You have no play here, but I'll tell you." He cleared his throat again. "She has been involuntarily committed to a seventy-two-hour suicide watch at the hospital, where she is undergoing therapeutic help. But the better question is, who are you, and how do you know her? Or better yet, how do you know me? Yesterday you said something about knowing what I was up to." His grin was wide enough to show pretty white teeth. "Pray tell. What the hell do you know about anything I do, stranger?"

She weighed the odds of walking out of the Twisted Tomato without incident, but she didn't think Barry would let that happen. He wanted to know about her so bad that he would arrest her on some trumped-up charge. She was stuck with him until he was satisfied, for better or worse, which angered her. Nobody held anything above her, especially not a threat.

"Did you know a baby is born with over three hundred bones?" Sarah said. "As a full-grown adult, we're at two hundred and six bones."

He shook his head briefly and leaned back in his seat. "What has that got to do with anything?"

"Just because you have a badge and are a member of the street gang in blue does not exempt you from learning a lesson. I'm looking across the table at a man. A simple man who bleeds." She tightened her jaw and spoke through her teeth. "If you've hurt Lesley in some way, I will break at least a dozen of your over two hundred bones." She leaned across the table and rested on her elbows. Lowering her voice, she said, "See how much respect I have for your badge? Only good people who protect and serve should ever wear that badge. Not men like you."

She was going out on a limb, but as the antagonizer, this fit right in.

"Threatening me? I've now got enough to arrest you. You've just made my day."

"Go ahead then. Arrest me, asshole. At my arraignment, I'll tell them what you've been up to, you piece of shit." She saw the first nervous tic on his face. He was guilty of something. That was why he was here, and Lesley wasn't. "You are so stupid. You should be thinking of ways to silence me, not bring me to the Queen's nest with the bee poison. I thought I was sitting across the table from a schooled man, a learned man. You're a joke with a badge who needs his friends to back him up at a meeting with a little girl like me." She shook her head and looked down at her hands. "Wow, did I ever overestimate you."

He didn't speak for a moment. Before he had a chance to respond, the waitress brought his coffee. She set it down and walked away. He dropped Aspartame-laced sweetener in his coffee and added cream.

"Aspartame and bovine growth hormone," Sarah said. "Bad mix."

"What?"

"Bovine growth hormone has been linked to increased breast and prostate cancer in recent years. Aspartame is horrible for … anyway, it doesn't matter here. Drink up."

"Okay, let's stop with the games," Barry said. "Who are you and what do you want?"

"You'll find out soon enough."

"No. I need to know what's going on." He finished stirring his coffee and lifted it to his lips, covering his mouth. "And you're going to tell me, or I will arrest you, and you won't make it to the police station for your interrogation. You'll learn a private lesson from an experienced Kelowna cop. Would you like that?"

He said the last part behind his coffee cup so no one could read his lips, and he spoke quietly enough that his backup couldn't even hear him.

"It doesn't matter what I say to you right now. You will keep on doing it until you're caught. You're like a fucking caterpillar."

"A what?" He set his coffee cup down. "A caterpillar?"

"If you place caterpillars on a circular path, they continue walking in circles until they die. That's you. The only difference is you set yourself on your own circular path. You set yourself up. Once you start, you can't stop, and it will kill you."

He narrowed those dead eyes of his. "Oh, you think you're so smart. So tell me, Miss Smarty Pants, what am I doing that'll kill me?"

"The fact that you came here today tells me so much about you. You're afraid of me. You wanted this setting, a public restaurant, with backup"—she glanced at the two men eating soup and a sandwich and gave them the finger—"because you're too afraid to take me downtown to talk." She turned back to Barry. "If they found out what you've been up to …" She let her voice trail off.

He sipped his coffee again. She tried to see if his hands were shaking, but they weren't.

"You thought you could bully me, harass me," Sarah continued. "But all you've done is confirmed my suspicions. You know," she waved a finger at him, "you shouldn't overthink this. Just roll with it because I'm not going away."

"All these subtle threats. Just tell me what you want, and stop dancing around with bullshit."

"You have overanalyzed this situation because you're afraid of what would happen if you weren't prepared, but you didn't expect something."

She had his full attention. He stared at her with those empty eyes, his hands wrapped around the mug of coffee.

"What didn't I expect?"

"Me." She leaned on her elbows. "People will hate you, try to break you, and shake your will. How strong you stand is what makes you. In the darkness, even your own shadow leaves you. I never depend on anyone but myself." She leaned back and dropped her arms to her side. Slowly, without moving her upper arm, she pulled the dog spray out of her pocket, flipped the safety off the top, then rested her thumb on the button, ready to shoot the spray. "You see, Barry Ashford, you're a problem for me, and sometimes the best way to solve a problem is to stop caring. Right now, I don't care about you, which makes me extremely dangerous. Not only do I *not* trust cops, I fucking hate them. So there's that, too."

They stared at each other. She waited for him to make a move, say something, or leave. But he just stared back at her with no expression.

"Fuck you." She pushed out of the booth. "I'm leaving."

Out of the corner of her eye, she caught the subtle movement of his head. He had nodded to his backup.

The two men pushed out their chairs and rushed her.

"Hey, who are you?" she yelled loud enough for all the patrons to hear. "Get off me," she shouted louder. By now, the entire restaurant had turned to face them. Neither man had identified themselves as police officers. One was pinning her arm behind her back while the other was trying to secure the arm with the dog spray.

She screamed for help as they pushed and started dragging her toward the restaurant's back. As she brought the spray around and aimed it over her shoulder at one of their faces, she caught Barry sipping his coffee as if he hadn't noticed what was happening two feet away.

As she released the spray, the man holding her arm howled and let go as he fell to the floor, clutching his face.

Sarah sprayed the other man from less than a foot away. For the benefit of the public, who sat transfixed by the violence, Sarah shouted, "That'll teach you for trying to manhandle me." With a harried, scared look, she viewed the other patrons to ensure they saw a small, terrified girl.

"Put it down," Barry said loud enough to be heard over the wounded cries of his colleagues.

He had a police issue sidearm aimed at her. She dropped

the dog spray.

"Oh, good," Sarah said. "The police. I want to press charges. Those two men tried to kidnap me."

"I saw the whole thing," a man added from the next booth.

A bearded man, three booths up, nodded. "I saw it, too." He had a cell phone in his hand.

"Those men on the floor are police officers," Barry shouted.

"What?" Sarah said, trying to look confused. "Then why didn't they identify themselves before they tried to haul me into the back room? Am I under arrest or something?"

A few patrons had gotten to their feet but hadn't moved any closer. They probably wouldn't while Barry held a gun.

"You are now. Turn around and assume the position. Hands on your head."

"On what charge?"

"Assaulting a peace officer and resisting arrest, to name a few. Now turn around."

"I didn't know I was being arrested until just now, and how was I supposed to know they were police officers dressed in civilian clothes and eating here like the rest of us?"

"Yeah," the bearded man said. He had his cell phone aimed at Barry. "I'm sick of police brutality in Kelowna. You're on tape, and I'll post to YouTube as soon as we're done here. Unless you want to arrest me and confiscate my phone, you're going to be famous."

Things had devolved quickly. Barry was at the losing end. His choice was simple: make a play for her or walk away.

His jaw muscles flexed. Then he raised his gun and aimed it at the ceiling.

"Okay, okay, true, no one identified themselves." He slipped his gun away.

"I want to press charges," Sarah said loud enough for everyone to hear. "These two men grabbed me and forcefully tried to drag me into the back room. I have no idea why they did that, but I want them arrested for attempting to abduct me."

Barry slid out of the booth and bent over to help one of the men up. Before reaching for the other man, he turned to Sarah. "Don't push me. Not now. Not here."

Low enough that only he could hear, she whispered, "You have no idea what I have in store for you. The end is near, and I'm the judge, jury, and executioner. You're through in Kelowna, and I'm the only one who can authorize your transfer … to jail."

Chapter 6

WHEN BARRY HAD HELPED his colleagues to the restaurant's bathroom to rinse their faces, Sarah thanked the bearded man for filming the event and ran out the back door. She ran through an alley and detoured down a side street until she felt safe from police harassment. Barry had been acting independently of the RCMP except for his friends, who likely came as a favor to him. He probably wasn't intending to arrest her, just get her outside, alone, where he would press her for more details.

She needed to clear the area, regroup, then decide how to come back at him. She had parked her bike by the beach. The sun had dropped farther during her time inside the Twisted Tomato, but it was still very warm out this summer evening. It surprised her that Barry would try to take her in public. He was more desperate than she thought, willing to take risks.

The scene he made at the restaurant motivated her to do

more to antagonize Barry one-on-one. It had to be when he didn't have backup when he was alone.

Keeping the fact that she was his neighbor from him would work to her advantage. Tonight, when he got home, and their lights went out for the evening, she would affix the GPS tracker to his vehicle, and tomorrow she would follow him with her cell phone. Learning what Barry spent his days doing could prove pivotal in discerning his illegal activities.

She located her bike without incident, revved the engine, merged into traffic, and headed home. So far, Barry hadn't gotten a good look at her bike, so she didn't need to worry about him recognizing it in her driveway. Even so, she would park it by the fence between the two properties, keeping it mostly out of sight.

As she passed the Twisted Tomato on Bernard Avenue, a Castanet van was parked out front.

Holy shit, are they everywhere?

It appeared Barry Ashford would be on the news twice in two days.

Which was a good thing. It would rattle him more.

When Sarah got home, she would find out where they would likely take Lesley for her suicide watch and see if she could find a way to gain access. It was imperative to discover Lesley's connection to Barry. After talking to Lesley, maybe an internet search would turn up something. Perhaps Castanet would have old news about Barry or his arrests.

Up ahead, someone had pushed the crosswalk button. The lights flickered on and off. A man started across the street.

Sarah slowed the bike, then lowered her leg to rest on an angle until the pedestrian cleared the road. In her mirror, a black Cadillac pulled up behind her.

The pedestrian got to the sidewalk.

She revved the bike and accelerated to the speed of traffic. The Caddy stayed close. At Glenmore, she stayed in the right lane even though she needed to turn left. At the last moment, as the light changed to yellow, she swung a hard left, dipping the bike low, and raced through the intersection, blocking any chance for the Cadillac to follow.

Heading north on Glenmore, she glanced in her mirror. The Caddy must have performed a U-turn because he was behind her and gaining.

She increased her speed, trying to keep some kind of distance between her and the Cadillac, which wasn't a police-issued vehicle.

Who knew she was in Kelowna? Who would be following her? More of Barry's friends? If so, she couldn't lead them to her house.

She came upon a small strip mall with a pub at the end. She parked in the farthest spot, jumped off the bike, and removed her helmet. The Caddy was just entering the parking lot by the time she set her helmet on the bike's seat. She had no weapons after leaving the dog spray at the Twisted Tomato.

The driver didn't falter or turn around after having been made. He continued to follow her and even pulled up and parked beside her bike. The driver appeared to be alone, but she couldn't see through the tinted back window.

Sarah ran along the side of the Cadillac and glanced in at the empty back seat. The car shut off, and the door clicked open. Sarah rested a hand on the door's glass as she looked inside to ensure he didn't have a weapon.

"Who are you, and why are you following me?" she asked, the door sitting open an inch.

"I'm not the enemy. I'm here to help."

"I'll decide that. Don't try to get out of the car. Name first?"

"Greg Wright. I'm Lesley's brother. I'm here to help. She told me to meet you tonight, but that asshole cop beat me to you."

Sarah let go of the door, and Greg stepped out. He was a tall man in his early twenties and extremely fit. His arms were cut as if molded from marble, and his chest was so solid it almost looked like he wore two armored plates over his pectorals.

"What do you know about Barry Ashford?" Sarah asked. She'd wanted to say, "Work out much?"

"Everything."

"Then let's go have a drink in this pub. You can tell me all about him."

Chapter 7

THEY SETTLED IN THE pub, Greg with a coffee and Sarah with an herbal tea.

"Why follow me?" Sarah asked. "That's risky. There are easier ways to catch my attention. You were parked by the beach. You saw me get on my bike. Why not get my attention there?"

"I needed to ensure Barry wasn't tailing you or had someone else watching you."

"I like caution." She pulled the tea bag, set it on the side, and wrapped her hands around the mug. "What can you tell me?' she asked.

He turned in his seat to see if anyone was paying attention to them. "Barry is into drugs."

Drugs? Vivian, you sent me here to deal with narcotics?

"What kind of drugs?"

"Heroin."

"Okay. Why tell me? Why not go to the police?"

"He is the police. And my sister understood that you and I knew one another."

Sarah let go of her mug and leaned back. "She must've gotten that impression from me at the beach."

"She thinks you can make it all go away."

"Whatever it is, I'm pretty sure I can."

"How?"

"That's my business." She looked around the pub and then met his eyes. "Before I'm done in Kelowna, Barry Ashford will pay for what he has done."

"That's why I'm here. Lesley said I could trust you, but I don't know you."

"You can trust me. You followed me, remember? You had already decided to trust me. So talk to me."

"Barry calls it flash-blooding."

"Calls what?"

"His heroin game."

Greg slurped his coffee and looked around again, his eyes darting back and forth nervously.

"Go on."

"I don't know much about how it started or who is involved, but I know my sister and I are. He's got us in tight. We must do what he says, or he'll lock us up."

"How? For what? He's not God. He doesn't own Kelowna. He's just a man with a badge."

"He's got something on us that won't go away."

"What is it?"

He looked down at the table as he fidgeted with a napkin. "Maybe later."

There was a moment of silent tension. Sarah waited.

"The local cops have their hands in different businesses." He tapped his foot on the base of the table. His hands tapped the table in rhythm with his foot. "Everyone on the street knows Barry owns some of the girls at the Garden of Eden Massage studio in town. He supplies the drugs, and the girls stay happy. When raids are scheduled, the girls get a heads-up. Nothing ever comes of it, and the public is mollified."

"Wow, Barry sounds like a busy man."

"Barry got into the drug scene too much a few years ago and started flash-blooding with a small group of people."

"Wait," Sarah held up a hand. "How do you know so much about the girls he owns at this massage studio and his drug group? Are you a part of it? Is that what he has on you?"

Greg checked the pub out again as if he was afraid Barry himself would enter through the back door with SWAT guns ready to execute him.

"My sister was down on her luck a few years ago. She thought she'd spend a summer doing massages. When she started at the Garden of Eden, she had no idea it was a full-service massage studio." He stopped tapping his hand and leaned across the table. "Anything goes. The rates they charge are based on what the customer is looking for. On her second day, she was ready to quit. There's no money in just doing massages. Then she met Barry. He told her he was a cop and that he would protect her. He handed her a thousand bucks and a little smack to take the edge off. Then he warned her. Leave the massage parlor and get arrested for prostitution and a whole slew of charges." Greg wiped his eyes. 'So my sister stayed that summer."

"I'm sorry to hear that." Sarah leaned across the table and touched his forearm, happy Aaron wasn't here. Aaron's sister had been murdered at a strip club in Toronto. If he were here, he would probably kill Barry Ashford with his bare hands. Sarah let go of Greg's arm and whispered just loud enough for him to hear, "Barry needs to be hurt. Bad."

Greg nodded. He sipped his coffee, took a deep breath, let it out, and collected himself.

"He filled her with drugs and kept her high that whole summer while …" he trailed off. Then said, "While he raped her repeatedly. She'll never be the same."

Sarah tightened her hand into a fist. Only swear words came to mind, but she kept her mouth closed. Greg needed comfort, not anger. The only way to rehabilitate men like Barry was to kill them. Then they'd learn. Once they were dead, they'd understand what they had done and how they had hurt others. At least, that was what Sarah told herself to justify Barry's murder.

"That's how flash-blooding works," Greg said.

"I think I'm lost. Explain how it works again."

He lowered his head and leaned in conspiratorially. "Barry shoots smack directly into one of the girl's veins, and then after five seconds, when the initial hit takes over, he withdraws her blood, laced with heroin, and injects that blood into the other girls, so they get high, too. A cost-effective way to share the drug without all the girls getting their own."

"They share blood laced with that shit? And the other girls get high as well? Just from the blood?"

Greg nodded. "Then he rapes them when they're high and spaced out. He calls it flash-blooding, and he also calls it his private H.O.—Heroin Orgies. The few girls at the parlor participating don't want the sex, but they can't say no to the free heroin. They're having sex with multiple men all day anyway, so why not bed their boss down as long as the heroin doesn't dry up? They're all addicted now. The only way out is rehab or what Lesley tried to do on the bridge yesterday."

"Are you saying Lesley still does this with Barry?"

Greg stopped tapping his foot under the table. His fingers fidgeted with themselves. "Yes, but at first, she got out. Called me last summer scared. Told me everything. I threatened to blow the whole thing sky-high. Tell the papers, tell the public. I got Lesley into rehab. Then a rash of break-and-enters happened across Kelowna, my head office included."

"ReadyMaid House Cleaning?"

A look of surprise crossed his face. "How did you know?"

"I met Derek earlier today and hired ReadyMaid to come to my house. What happened with the break-ins?"

"I can't prove this, but I think Barry targeted my office and then broke into homes on my client list. He focused on those homes—"

Sarah held up a hand for him to stop. "He broke into the homes that didn't have an alarm. Those people who left a key outside for the cleaner to enter when they were at work or away."

His eyebrows lowered and connected above the bridge of his nose. "How did you know that?"

"Derek gave my house a walk-through. He asked questions about my alarm system and whether I would be willing to leave a key outside. It wasn't a stretch to put it together."

Greg shook his head as if he had to clear it. "Okay, well,

Barry targeted these houses. The break-ins were never solved as there was no forced entry. They suspected me, but Barry offered a weak alibi for me. If I say anything negative about him, he will recant the alibi. Barry ensured I knew everything and that he would pin the whole thing on my company and me. I was told that my company, which I had built over the past ten years, would be shut down, and I would lose everything and eventually go to jail. And that wasn't the worst part."

"Really? What else is there?" Sarah sipped her tea, which had grown cold.

"Maxine Freeman went missing eight months ago. She was part of the flash-blooders. One day she was there, complaining about Barry, and the next day, she had skipped town. I found it suspicious, but I didn't see a missing persons report in the newspaper or anything. Then, two weeks later, I bumped into her brother at the mall, and he said she was missing, as in disappeared. Last seen getting into Barry's car. When Maxine's brother called the police, Officer Ashford said he knew her and that she said she was heading to Halifax. Apparently, he had driven her to the bus station himself. No one has heard from Maxine since. My sister and I think she's dead."

Sarah leaned back in her chair. "This only gets worse."

"Barry told Lesley that if she didn't return to the Garden and rejoin the party, she would have to go to 'Halifax' like Maxine." He used air quotes on Halifax. "Lesley is so scared … well, you saw what she tried to do yesterday."

Greg shuddered. His other leg bounced up and down now. He hadn't drunk much of his coffee.

"I'm so sorry," Sarah said.

The pub's front door opened. Two uniformed officers entered.

"Don't look now, but two cops just came in. Probably unrelated. Looks like they're heading to a table to sit and eat."

"I gotta go," Greg said, panic in his voice. "I can't be seen with you."

"Why not? We're just a man and a woman having a drink."

"If it gets back to Barry that we talked, Lesley's dead, and if he doesn't kill me, he'll ruin my life, which will kill me."

"Is he still breaking into homes?"

"Not that I know of. But he says he planted evidence in some of the homes. It's something he can pull out later if he needs to." Greg glanced over his shoulder. "Look, I gotta go. Can you help us?" Fear sparked in his eyes.

"Yes," she said, unsure how, but she trusted Vivian.

That one word calmed him visibly.

He slid out of his chair and stood. "Thanks. I'm sure we'll be in touch. You know where to find me."

He walked past her and headed for the side door, so he didn't have to walk by the cops.

After a moment, Sarah paid the bill and walked out to her bike.

Officer Ashford had to be held accountable for his disgusting crimes, and there was only one way Sarah could think of nailing him.

She would watch him for twenty-four hours using her GPS tracking device. Then she would abduct him and force him to confess under pain of torture.

The nightmare would be over for Lesley and all the girls he had been raping.

How ironic.

It was a cop who had violated Sarah when she was a preteen. She hated all cops after that and started pulling her hair out, eventually falling into a deep depression that lasted years until Vivian began talking through her.

Funny how life came full circle.

She hated men like Barry. He couldn't be allowed to exist. He was cancer in an otherwise healthy society.

And it was time to excise that particular cancer.

She got on her bike and pulled out of the pub's parking lot, revving her bike's engine in anger.

Barry Ashford was in for a world of pain. Lucky Sarah would get the pleasure of exacting it.

This is going to be fun.

Chapter 8

"YOU HAVE GOT TO be kidding me!" Deborah shouted. "Are you saying some bitch showed up out of nowhere and claimed to know who you are and what you've been up to, and you haven't dealt with it yet? And you don't even know where she is?"

"Yep, that's it." Barry leaned on the kitchen counter, both hands tightened into fists. After cleaning up at the restaurant, his colleagues left him there, but not before expressing how pissed they were at him. He owed them big time for what happened. The situation with the strange girl had gotten out of hand. He didn't know where it was headed and had no idea how to stop it.

"You see? That's what I said last night." She threw back the rest of her wine into her mouth, swallowed, and set the goblet down beside his hands. "We need to leave. Get out while the gettin's good." She belched in his ear. It always disgusted him, but she did it anyway. "Do you have any better ideas? Should I start packing?"

He pushed off the counter and punched the cupboard by her face. Deborah jumped. "Do. Not. Pack. Anything. I will not be driven from my city or home." He pointed at her. "I will find out who this stranger is and what she wants, and if she doesn't fuck off, I will bury her in a dumpster somewhere before I leave with my tail between my legs."

Debbie stepped back to place the island between them. She leaned against the fridge. "Be careful what you say. When you got into the whorehouse business, I objected. But you won me over with all the cash. It paid for all this." She raised her hands like a girl on the *Price is Right*, showing off the new house he could win. "I know about the drugs, too. I'm not stupid. Those girls need to be jacked up to have sex a dozen times a day with a dozen different men. I get it." She lowered her eyes and looked away. "I lost my husband when you started this project."

"Oh, come on, honey," he said in a softer voice.

Her head snapped up. "Don't try to placate me. I know about the heroin parties. You come home smelling like pussy. Don't worry. I sold my soul to the devil just as much as you did because I didn't want the money to stop flowing. The only thing I ever worried about was you falling in love with one of those young hot bimbos whose tits still sit straight up. Not like these." She held her breasts for a second, bouncing them. "Then I saw you with that Maxine Freeman girl."

"You what?"

"I saw you. She was in your car."

He thought back to the last day he saw Maxine. He had driven her to the bus depot. She wanted a ticket to a city as far from Kelowna as possible. That was their deal. Go quietly or end up in jail. She chose Halifax. He never saw her again.

"She's gone," he said. "If you saw her in my car, it was because I was driving her to the bus station."

"Yeah, well, whatever. I just thought I would be replaced one day. So I saved up some money."

His anger returned. "How much money are we talking about?"

"Enough to get out of Kelowna. Start fresh in another city. Maybe another country. I've been doing some research. There's a country in the Caribbean called St. Kitts where you can buy a house worth four hundred thousand or more, and they'll give you a passport. You can literally buy citizenship there. We could retire to the beach in the Caribbean and revoke our Canadian passports. But that's not all. St. Kitts doesn't have any tax. No sales tax and no income tax. We retire. You collect whatever pension you have, and we live happily ever after, never to do a tax return again. How does that sound?" She moved closer, trying to soothe and coo an answer out of him. "Would you like that, honey?"

Manipulation, coercion, and the beguiling smile from his wife incensed him. He formed a fist. All the stress of the last two days coursed through his knuckles. They tingled with the need to connect with something. For a brief moment, that annoying girl's face flashed before his eyes, and before he knew what he was doing, Barry drove his fist into Deborah's cheek so hard she lifted off her feet. Her body floated completely parallel to the floor for a brief moment before landing on her back. The hard landing knocked the wind out of her, her cheek already bleeding.

"You *stupid* bitch!" he screamed. "How dare you save *my*

money without telling me. How long have you been setting up this little escape plan of yours? Huh? Tell me! Were you going to run away on me and take all my money?"

He leaned over her squirming form on the floor, hating her for everything she was, spitting on her as he shouted. All she ever did was shop at the mall and then sit around the house and drink red wine. When he came home from work, she would harass him about what he was doing with his other ventures and offer unsolicited advice on how to do things better, all in the name of maintaining the freedom to shop all day and drink more wine.

"How dare you!" he shouted again. "It would've been better if you had kept your mouth shut and just thanked me when I gave you your month's budget."

He straightened and swung his arm across the counter, knocking her juicer to the floor. "Goodbye, juicer." He grabbed the cord to the rice steamer she had bought at Costco and yanked it to the floor. "No more rice cooker."

Deborah screamed for him to stop. "Please, I'm sorry!"

"You have everything you could possibly want. You're still unhappy with all the money, the shopping, and the booze. There's nothing I can do to please you, is there? No nice home, loaded with everything most women would kill for. No fancy car or vacations. No, you want to escape this wonderful life. You want to run at the first sign of trouble. One snotty, big-mouthed girl has gotten in my way. That's all this is. I will remove her. The stain will be taken out. Everything is normal, and we must act as though it is."

"I know," Debbie said as she leaned against the cupboard, holding her cheek. A small amount of blood seeped through her fingers, and her eyes were wet with tears.

"I'm sorry. You're right. I should be more grateful."

"Fuckin' right."

He grabbed a paper towel and wiped his knuckles, then the moisture from his face.

"I've got an officer friend coming over during his night shift, somewhere around two in the morning. I'm giving him a description of this lunatic woman. We're going to finish this tomorrow at the latest. Soon I'll have every cop looking for her. Once she's gone, it'll be business as usual."

"What about Lesley?"

"What? You don't think I handled that?"

"Yes, of course you did."

"She has been warned, and so has her brother. There's nothing they can do or will do. Lesley comes back to work tomorrow, and then we'll see." He stared out the kitchen window into the dark night. "Maybe she just needs an extra dose of smack." He turned to Deborah as an idea came to him. ' She has already proven she wants to end her life. Once she overdoses, I'll have one of the other girls find her. Problem solved."

"And Greg, her brother? He'll become a problem."

"I'll issue an arrest warrant for him in the morning. We'll raid his business and clean him out. I know the judge, and I'll do my damnedest to make sure he doesn't get bail. We'll see what stories he has while stuck in prison. No one will believe shit because he'll be trying to smear the cop who put him away. Does that make you happy? That annoying bitch goes away, and Greg and Lesley Wright get dealt with. Do we still need to run with our tails between our legs? Huh?"

Debbie shook her head back and forth. "I was thinking about you and your safety." She took a Kleenex off the counter and held it to her face. "Can you really kill someone?" she asked softly.

"I'm not killing anyone. The smack is. I'm just helping her have the ride of her life." He kicked chunks of plastic pieces from the rice cooker's lid out of his way and headed for the fridge. He pulled a beer, twisted off the cap, and drank it back. "The answer is yes." He felt a pulse behind his eyes. "Yes, I would kill another human being with my bare hands to protect us. If it was me going down or them, it'll always be them. That includes you." He pulled hard on the beer. "Don't forget that."

He turned away from the disgusting look on his wife's face and left the kitchen. If he hadn't, he would've punched her again.

But if he started hitting her, he was afraid he wouldn't be able to stop.

Chapter 9

In her kitchen, peeking out the window with the lights turned off, Sarah sipped a glass of Mission Hill shiraz from a local winery. It was almost two in the morning, and the last of the lights at the Ashford house had gone out half an hour ago. She would wait ten more minutes and then head outside to plant the tracker under Barry's front fender or behind the grill, wherever she found the best purchase.

Deborah's car was the cute Volkswagen Bug. As Sarah had hoped, Barry had driven home in an unmarked cruiser. He had backed in, parking in front of Deborah's car so he would be the one to leave first.

Sarah closed the curtains in her dark kitchen and headed back downstairs. She had moved the furniture into the spare room and cleared the floor space in the center of the basement. The carpet had been difficult to roll up on her own, but she managed it and exposed a six-foot square area of concrete.

Now, if blood spilled on it, cleaning it would be easier. Then the carpet could be rolled back in place, and the furniture set on top of that. No one would ever know what she had done.

No one except Barry Ashford.

She closed the vents so none of the cold air from the conditioner would reach the basement. When he arrived, he needed to sweat.

She checked that the chair in the center of the floor was secure and that her floor lamp was aimed at the chair. When Barry confessed to whatever he had been up to, she would see his face, and so would the small nanny camera and digital video recorder she had bought at Spy vs. Spy. It only recorded when it detected movement, and the memory on the DVR was enough to handle a couple of weeks, but his confession would only take a day or two.

The camera was hidden in a wall clock. The camera's lens sat at the base of the number six in the clock. She had affixed it to the wall beside the basement closet. Tiny wires fed to the DVR on the top shelf in the closet, unseen by anyone unless they opened the closet door and knew what they were looking for.

Now that everything was in place, she turned off the lights and closed her eyes tight. She waited until her eyes adjusted to the dark and headed upstairs. Once the GPS tracker was turned on and her cell phone had locked in on the signal, she placed it in the container with the highly magnetized exterior. Then she donned a black jacket, gloves, and a hat and slipped out her back door.

As she listened to the sounds of the night, nothing odd

stood out. Waves lapped the docks at Okanagan Lake below. An engine revved somewhere far away. Crickets shouted their mating call. Nothing seemed out of place. The air was still and warm. Sweat moistened her hat around the brim.

She crept around the house and along her driveway. She stopped at the edge of the property fence and stared at the dark front of the Ashford house. The curtains were pulled shut. Nothing moved.

Her house was the second to the last, and the Rankins' house was at the end of their street. Bennett Road wasn't a thoroughfare. The only traffic this far down was heading to one of these three houses. The Rankins weren't home, and the Ashfords were asleep. Since no one visited Sarah or even knew where she lived, she didn't expect any interruptions.

Sarah stepped out from the cover of the fence and headed for Barry's unmarked RCMP cruiser, watching their front windows for movement or light. She crossed the distance silently, the black socks she wore to keep noise to a minimum doing exactly that.

She walked around to the front of the vehicle and looked at the street behind her.

Empty.

She ducked down to the level of the hood, then stopped.

Something had caught her eye by the Ashford's front door. She stared, waiting it out.

What had moved?

Then she saw it again. A cigarette. The glow of the heater was at the tip as someone pulled on the smoke.

Someone was standing outside their front door, smoking.

How did they not see me?

She counted her lucky stars. She was here now. Plant the

GPS tracker and crawl away. It was a strategic advantage to live next door to Barry and not have him know that yet. Blowing it because of carelessness would be tragic.

Slowly, making sure she didn't drop the box in her hand or bang the car's grill needlessly, Sarah got down on her back and edged under the front of the car. Blind in the dark, she felt around behind the grill for a safe place to clamp the box. After a few surfaces proved too small, she decided to place it on the inside of the fender. A tiny spot just above the lower lip in front of the axle had just enough room for the magnetized box.

As soon as the magnets took hold, it would smack down. She took her time, using both hands, and carefully brought the box close to the spot, waiting for the pull of the magnets.

A car's engine revved, this time closer. She waited a moment, listening for another loud report from the engine. When it came, she brought the box up to the metal and felt it snap forward, attaching itself to the car.

Her job was done.

She edged her head out from under Barry's car and rolled onto her stomach. The car that had revved its engine was getting closer. Its headlights cast their extended beam along the dead-end road.

Shit.

Footsteps drew close. Whoever had been smoking by the front door of the Ashford's house had been waiting for someone to show up. Now that person was walking beside Barry's unmarked cruiser.

The approaching car was one house away as Sarah rolled around the front of the cruiser and leaned against the passenger side door. She curled her knees up to her chest and wrapped her arms around her legs to make herself unseen as the headlights swung into Barry's driveway. They flashed across her black form so fast she was sure the driver didn't see her in the dark.

A door opened. "Barry, you doing okay?" the driver asked.

Sarah saw enough of the car to know it was an RCMP cruiser.

"Yeah, Colin," Barry said. "I just need your help with something."

The car door shut as Colin walked around the front. As he passed each headlight, it blinked out for a second.

"Anything. You know that."

Sarah lifted up to see both men. They embraced, patted each other's backs, and then stepped back.

"I've got a problem," Barry said.

"Your problem is my problem, brother."

"That's why I called you."

"Remember that biker's cocaine lab we busted?"

Barry nodded. In the headlights of the car, Sarah saw Barry's face clearly.

"What a day that was," Colin said. "Remember how we'd cleared the rooms? Everyone was accounted for. But that big fucker got a gun somehow and shot at us."

Barry nodded and placed a hand on Colin's shoulder. "I was there."

"You had a cool head. I froze. You pulled your weapon. I shit my pants. You fired and hit his shoulder and stomach. I fired piss into my shorts. He went down, and you saved my life. I was a dead man if I hadn't been standing beside you. There are not many men who I'd clear a room with, but you're one of them."

"I know. And I appreciate that."

"I owe you more than I can ever repay. Tell me what you need and consider it done."

"I need one girl arrested."

"What's she done, and why don't you arrest her yourself?"

"She's annoying the shit out of me. Harassing me. And I can't arrest her myself because she's trying to make a case against me."

"A case? How?"

"Castanet has seen me with her twice, and each time she turns out to look like the good guy. If I arrest her, I don't think the charges will stick."

Barry told Colin about saving the attempted suicide and how Sarah had shown up and talked shit. Then she interrupted his dinner with two other members of the force and pepper sprayed them.

"I heard about that. What the fuck, man? Who is this woman?"

"I don't know a thing about her. I just met her yesterday, and she won't tell me what she's up to. All she does is show up and direct her pissy attitude at me. I'm trying to do the right thing here."

"Why didn't you arrest her at the Tomato when she sprayed you guys?" Colin asked.

"Because she made it look like police brutality. Some asshole was filming it. We didn't identify ourselves right away. It sounds like she knows the law, too. I just don't get it."

"Tell me what she looks like."

Barry described her to Colin as Sarah's knees protested her scrunched position. Sweat rolled down her forehead. If she moved, they would see her. The only plus was the cruiser's engine still idled, which would cover any minor noise she made.

"I'll let some of the guys know to keep an eye out for her.'

"And Colin." Barry put a hand on Colin's shoulder again. "Once she's off the street, come on by the Garden. I'll send three girls into your room this time, free of charge."

"You don't have to," Colin protested.

"No. I do. It's my way of thanking you."

"Just send in that Lesley girl. She's the one I want."

"Oh, I can't." Barry tapped his lower lip with his finger as if he were contemplating something important. "After what happened at the bridge, I think she will have to take a leave of absence." He stopped tapping his lip. "A permanent one."

"However you run your business is up to you. Not many employers can get away with firing someone for attempted suicide, but you can. I know some of the guys are going to miss her."

"I think she's been passed around a little too much anyway."

Sarah felt like throwing up. Either that or stand up and murder both men in an uncontrolled rage. Her stomach clenched, and she almost coughed. She prayed for Lesley and thanked Vivian for sending her here. The Garden of Eden would be closed for business by the end of the week if Sarah had anything to do with it.

The men embraced again.

"Oh, and Colin, she rides a motorcycle. I think it's a BMW, but I'm not sure. I've only seen it from a distance."

Colin got in his cruiser. When he pulled out, he swung the nose of the car the other way, sparing the headlight glare flashing across her position.

Moments later, as his engine noise faded in the distance and Sarah's knees were aflame, Barry slowly made his way back up his driveway.

His front door opened and closed softly.

Sarah crawled to her fence, got up, and stumbled to her back door on cramped legs. Once inside, with the hat and gloves off, her hand went numb.

Vivian.

She grabbed a pen and paper and lay down on the living room floor, breathing steadily, trying to quell her pulse. She had no idea how she was going to sleep tonight.

Then she blacked out.

A few moments later, she woke to a note.

The exact spot where the remains of Maxine Freeman's body had been buried was written down.

Sarah was also told to be at the Garden of Eden studio at 3:17 p.m. tomorrow afternoon. She would know what to do, Vivian added.

Vivian said she was sorry, but this had to be done.

She also said she trusted Sarah to handle this task but to be prepared for a darker truth.

Sarah looked up at the ceiling. "Are you saying the drugs and the rape of all these women aren't all that I'm here for?"

She blacked out and came to seconds later, another note beside her hand.

The drugs and the rape are the barnacles on this mother

ship. You're in Kelowna to stop something much darker. I'm keeping it from you for a reason, but you'll learn what it is soon enough. For now, sleep. You'll need it.

"Shit," she mumbled to herself. "What's worse? What's a darker truth?"

Chapter 10

In the morning, Sarah made coffee and turned on her MacBook Pro to catch the news.

At the top of the list under the Kelowna tag, Castanet was reporting on the grisly findings of a human body in a wooded region off of Bear Creek Road. The body had been found in a garbage bag. There were unconfirmed reports that the body was female and that animals might have tampered with the remains. The BC Coroner's office would determine the cause of death after an autopsy over the next few days. Police were still scouring the area for more clues.

Before bed, Sarah had made an anonymous call to Castanet's phone lines to report that she had found something suspicious. After giving the directions supplied by Vivian, she hung up the phone and went to bed. That was five hours ago.

"At least now, Maxine Freeman will be able to rest in

peace," she said to herself.

Another report on Castanet showed a sketch artist's drawing of a woman the police were looking for. The article said that the woman had been involved in various crimes throughout the city. Anyone who saw this woman was directed to contact the police. A phone number was supplied.

The sketch artist's drawing resembled Sarah.

She scrolled down farther. Below the original article was another picture. This one was blurry but wasn't hard to make out. It was definitely Sarah.

"Shit. How did they get my picture?"

She saw the sand behind her in the image. Castanet had filmed her at the beach. Sarah had used it as a warning to Barry to keep him calm. He must've asked for their footage and then Photoshopped it enough to make it as clear as it was.

She would have to leave the house in disguise. Getting arrested would not work. She had to find out what Vivian meant by the darker truth. And she had to be at the Garden of Eden at 3:17 p.m.

After her shower, she dressed and got ready to go. She logged into the GPS tracker on Barry's vehicle and checked where it had gone and where it was now.

According to the tracker, he was parked a block from the downtown RCMP detachment. The history of Barry's travels revealed that he drove right there from home without stopping. This meant he probably called Castanet and asked for the picture, then drove to the station where he helped prepare it. This also meant that every police officer on the street was a threat, and they would be looking for a female on a BMW motorcycle.

She had to ditch the motorcycle. She would have to rent a car.

The number for Enterprise Car Rental was an easy one to find. She called them because their ad said they would pick her up at home.

After their standard greeting, Sarah said, "I need a car for a couple of days."

"Are you looking for small or mid-size?"

"Mid-size. SUV if you have it."

"You're in luck. We've got a Jeep Cherokee in from Alberta right now."

"Perfect. Hold that one for me."

"Done. Your name?"

"Sarah Roberts. And I'll need a pickup."

"No problem. Your address?"

"I'm out on Bennett Road in McKinley Landing."

"Oh, I'm sorry. That's on the outskirts of Kelowna and outside our pickup area. Is there any way you could get here on your own?"

Sarah sighed. "Yes. Just hold the Jeep. I'll be there in an hour or so."

A quick ride using side streets wouldn't be a problem. Not every street will be guarded by the cops.

Half an hour later, dressed in jeans, a heavy shirt, and a red baseball cap in her pocket, for when she took her helmet off, Sarah stepped outside, locked her door, and got on her bike.

She logged in on her cell phone to see where Barry's cruiser was and discovered that he was on the move. She watched his direction and tried to guess where he was heading. The Garden of Eden was on the north side of town, just off Harvey Avenue. Barry was on Glenmore heading north.

That could only mean one thing. He was coming home.

She would be housebound if he got here first.

She raced down Bennett Road and then along McKinley, which led out to Glenmore. It was the only way in and out of McKinley Landing. They would pass each other on the two-lane road if she didn't hit Glenmore before he came onto McKinley. Glenmore was also a two-way, but it had a center median. There would be distance between them. She could be just another passing cyclist, as far as he was concerned.

On the last curve before Glenmore, she pulled out her phone and checked his location. He was still two miles from McKinley Road.

At Glenmore, she turned right, heading into town. She would see his unmarked cruiser coming her way soon.

She came up to a green light at Union Street and waited in the left turn lane. Taking Union was a shortcut to the north side of Kelowna and would take her to the car rental place faster. It would also avoid driving toward and having to pass Barry's vehicle.

But the traffic didn't lighten up in time.

Barry's brown unmarked cruiser came into view, heading her way.

"Damn," she said under her helmet. "So close."

She waited at the light, her signal on. He entered the intersection and then passed her without looking over. When she could, Sarah took the turn as if she wasn't in a hurry and continued along Union until she took another left onto Sexsmith Road. In her mirrors, no one followed her.

She continued along the curvy Sexsmith, watching for

any sign that she was being tailed.

After a particularly long bend in the road, she straightened the bike, set her speed to five over the limit, and checked her mirrors.

An engine revved loud and clear through the helmet.

She snapped her head around.

It couldn't be.

Somehow Barry had made her, did a U-turn on Glenmore, and gave chase. Without her noticing, he caught up fast, which wasn't too hard as Sexsmith twisted and wound its way to the north part of town.

She sped up, knowing that she couldn't drive to Enterprise and get into the Jeep. She had to lose him first.

His sirens trilled once, then again. There was no way she would pull over for him, let alone on this back road where there would be no witnesses, and he was the only one armed.

She kept up her speed, but the corners slowed her down. He tried to overtake her once, coming very close to the shoulder of the road as she dipped into a turn.

"What the fuck are you trying to do?" she shouted under her helmet.

She snuck a quick look in her mirror as she prepared for another corner. A minivan came from the opposite direction. Just as it passed, she dipped for the corner and heard Barry's engine rev at the same time.

When she righted the bike, he was directly beside her. She looked through his passenger side window at him. She could read his intentions in those dead eyes.

He jerked on the wheel of his car, and the unmarked cruiser hopped to the right. The front right fender of Barry's cruiser smacked the bike. If Sarah hadn't lifted her left leg, it would've been crushed between his passenger door and her bike's engine.

The bike veered to the right, and for a brief second, she was sure she would fly off the edge. As she attempted to correct her steering while half on and half off the bike, her left leg still in the air, the front wheel wobbled back and forth. There was no way she could keep the bike on the road.

Past the point of no return, Sarah and her bike sailed over the lip of the shoulder and took air. The bike dropped below her as she released the handlebars and prepared to land and roll. The ground came fast, and with it, trees, stumps, and large rocks. The ground sloped at an angle away from the road. When she hit the grass, she rolled, twisted, and turned until she reached the bottom of the hill twenty feet below.

The wooden base of a thick pine tree connected with her helmet and ceased her descent.

It also ceased all cognitive thought.

Chapter 11

ONCE THE BIKE DISAPPEARED from view, Barry continued along Sexsmith Road as if nothing had happened. He adjusted himself in his seat, wiped his brow, and checked the mirrors to see if anyone had stopped to help the girl.

He made a U-turn three hundred yards away from the incident and started back to where the girl and her bike went over. He pulled up and looked down from the driver's side window. Her body was twisted at an impossible angle, her head hidden behind the base of a tree. It was as if she was in the middle of attempting a somersault. He wanted to walk down and wrap his hands around her throat until she gasped her last breath. But as he watched, she didn't move. She didn't even twitch.

Maybe she was already dead. If not, when she was discovered, she would end up in the hospital and then get arrested. He'd get his day.

A Hydro truck passed on the road beside him. There was no one else around. After the girl flew over the edge, no one had passed going either way until the truck.

He pushed the accelerator and pulled away.

"I hope you're dead," he said to himself.

At home, he parked behind his wife's Bug, got out, and breathed deep fresh air. It was good to be home. Good to have solved everything. The meddling girl was probably dead or would be hospitalized soon, and this afternoon he would deal with Lesley Wright. Anything of recent concern would go away, and life would return to normal soon enough.

The only thing left to deal with was his crazy wife. She knew too much and was threatening to leave him. She had to stay in Kelowna or be placed in a garbage bag and discarded as Maxine Freeman had been.

He had no idea how that happened to Maxine. He had left her at the bus depot. She was warned to never come back. Maxine's brother had asked him about his sister weeks later, but that was one time he didn't have to lie. He really did drop her off and let her go. She had been terrified of him. She had been tortured to a perpetual state of paranoia. She probably killed herself on Bear Creek Road and offered the coyotes and mountain lions dinner.

With that thought on his mind, he adjusted his jacket and entered the house.

"Deb, I'm home."

She didn't respond. A bottle of wine sat half empty on the kitchen counter.

What a fucking drunk.

The rocking chair on the deck squeaked. He grabbed a glass, poured himself some, and went to join her. As soon as he gave her a malefic warning, he would spend the afternoon flash-blooding at the Garden of Eden. He would enjoy himself at Lesley's expense until she passed out from too much in her system. Then the real fun would begin. His stomach twitched in anticipation at the wild afternoon he was going to have.

The sliding door hadn't closed fully when his wife started up.

"Now, what are we going to do?" she asked.

The cut on her face looked terrible, and her eyes were wounded and red. There was a moment when he felt pity but then brushed it aside.

Your blood is so thin from the alcohol you can't even heal normally.

He brought the wine to his lips, savored its taste, cleansed his palate, and swallowed. Then he did it again to really taste the wine. A nice shiraz.

Damn, it's good to be in control.

"What are you talking about?" He leaned on the deck's railing and stared out at Okanagan Lake. A water skier fanned back and forth behind a boat. Two jet skis raced each other.

"Maxine Freeman. I want to know how you did it."

He turned to her, offended she would just assume he killed her. "I'm many things, but I'm not a murderer of innocent women." *Although that changes today ...*

"Are you denying it? Even after I saw you with her that day? It has only been eight months. People will remember she worked at the Garden of Eden and that you two were close. Some people might even know that you drove her to the bus depot. That might make you the last person to see her alive, which is a big deal."

"Don't go witch hunting. You're always borrowing trouble." He pumped his hand in the air, open-palmed. "Just bring it down a notch."

"And what about Sarah?"

He squinted and looked sideways at her. "Who's Sarah?"

"The girl who lives next door."

He shook his head in confusion. "What? What are you talking about? Didn't a couple live there until a month ago or something? Jacob and his girlfriend?"

Deborah laughed and slapped her knee. "You see, this is why we're finished."

"Make sense, woman." He spread his arms out, almost spilling his wine. "Are you so drunk that you can't even talk straight to me?"

Her face darkened. She glared at him. "You want sense? Is that what you want?" She placed her wine glass on the wooden floor of the deck and stood. "You were the last one to see Maxine Freeman alive. You will have questions to answer regarding that. And this thing you're doing with Castanet, the girl's photo you circulated. Embarrassed much?" She slapped her hands together. "She lives next door. When everyone finds out you're looking for your neighbor and you didn't even know it, boy, talk about egg on your face —"

He shoved her. He couldn't listen to her condescending tone anymore. Or her disrespect. She had so much to learn, and this wasn't the way the lesson was supposed to go.

Debbie fell backward into her chair. Her sunglasses popped back and fell off her head. She squinted at him.

"What the hell was that for?" she asked.

But he didn't answer right away.

Next-door neighbor? What was she talking about?

"Just shut up and tell me more about this neighbor."

"Joan and Mike flew in to rent the place for a few more months. Luckily for them, they found a tenant. A writer. Her name is Sarah. I forget the last name. Haven't seen her since she moved in. Oh, I forgot, you're too busy to even notice me. Then I see her picture blasted in the paper today."

"What kind of vehicle does she have?"

"A motorcycle. I don't know much about vehicles, but I took a double-take of this one because BMW makes it. I had no idea before two days ago that BMW even makes motorcycles."

He leaned down close to her face, his hands on the armrests of her chair. "And why am I only hearing of this now?"

"You're kidding, right? Every time someone moves in or out of a house on this street, you need to be informed? Oh, right, you're king shit. I'm sorry. I forgot."

He slapped her face, careful to ensure he hit last night's wounded cheek. Better to double the pain than give her a new mark. But then he got carried away, and as she cried out, he slapped her back and forth until she hid her face in her lap, screaming hysterically.

He pulled up, breathing frantically. His hair fell in his eyes. He brushed it back, drank the rest of his wine, and waited until she got better control of herself.

After what felt like a full minute, she raised her head. Both cheeks were a deep red, with last night's wound bleeding again.

"You asshole," she breathed through her teeth.

"And then some. Disrespect me again, and I will fucking kill you and bury you in the bushes, but I'll do a better job than the amateurs who killed Maxine. I'll make sure coyotes find your body. They'll lick your bones clean."

She backhanded tears as they slipped from her eyes. "What happened to us?"

"Nothing. We're roommates now. I live my life, and you have a nice home, all the food you want, and enough money in your monthly budget that a certified electrician would kill to make. All you have to do is join me at police events and make your public appearances seem normal." He pushed his thumb and index finger together. "A little task for a big return. What happened to us is your greed. You always want more, and now that we're deep, you want to cut and run. Well, fuck that. We're not going anywhere, and neither are you. Understood?"

Debbie looked out at the water. "Fair enough. We'll do it your way. We won't run. Everything will work out. I'll be quiet and obey. It'll go back to how it was before Lesley tried to off herself. But don't hurt that girl next door. She's sweet and innocent. Leave her out of this."

"You're kidding now, aren't you?"

"What do you want her for, anyway? What has she done?"

He ignored her question. "Just know this. I'm done with things going wrong. I'm done with worrying about people who have big mouths. It's time to get stronger." He pointed a finger in her face. "Go back to normal. Act normal. Drink all you want. Kill yourself. I don't fucking care. But *never*," he shouted the last word, "ever, disrespect me again or plot against me. I will kill you and bury you in this house if I see ever the slightest bullshit from you. Understand?"

He caught what he thought was the edge of a smile on her face. He was about to respond when she lowered her head.

"I understand, and I'm sorry. This isn't the right time to add to your stress." She fiddled with her shirt, picking a piece of lint off it. "I deserved last night's punch and today's slaps. I've been out of line, and it won't happen again. We're in this together, thick and thin."

This surprised him, but he was suddenly very happy with her.

"Good. I'm glad you see it my way." He headed for the door. "I have to get back on the road. Business to attend to."

"Aren't you going next door to talk to Sarah or take her in?"

"She's not there," he said, half in the house, half on the deck.

"How do you know that?"

"She's in a ditch off Sexsmith Road. Bad accident." He looked down at his feet as if he was upset. "She took a spill on one of those corners, rolled down the embankment, and smacked a tree with her head." He met Debbie's eyes. "When I last saw her, she wasn't moving." He shrugged. "Looks like she won't be a problem anymore."

He stepped inside the house before Debbie could say anything.

What a victory today had started with. That meddling girl, Sarah, had been taken out. His wife had agreed to his terms, and now he was heading to the Garden of Eden to help Lesley with her suicide bid.

But first, Lesley was going to give him a going away

present.

Since Lesley wouldn't have any more customers today, or ever, he didn't need a condom. Unprotected sex with the drugged whores when they were too high to even know what was happening to them was his favorite. They all figured it out eventually, but he was a cop. Who were they going to tell? His friends? Before long, they needed more smack, and he was the only source of heroin in the Garden of Eden.

In a few hours, Lesley was going to be so high she would never know the horrific violations he would do because she would never wake up.

When they found her body and toxicology reports confirmed the overdose, the only issue would be his semen, but since he wasn't a registered sex offender, he was safe. If it ever came back to him, it wouldn't matter. He owned the place and slept with all the girls. It was part of their job description.

He was the one who would either investigate her death or be consulted on it. She was a sex worker, after all. Nobody would look too hard for a murderer when Lesley had tried to kill herself two days before. She came to work, had sex with multiple men, and then overdosed. That will be the story.

He stepped onto the front lawn, made his way to the car, and said out loud, for the benefit of the trees and the birds flitting around in their branches, "What a glorious day. It's shaping up to be a killer of a day."

Then he got in his car and headed to the Garden with a plan to drive by Sarah's accident location.

He wanted to take a peek at the rescue attempt.

If there was one.

Chapter 12

Greg Wright entered the Garden of Eden Massage Parlor faster than he intended. The door banged against the wall, startling the two girls sitting on the couch.

"Can we help you?" the tall one asked as she got to her feet.

It was hard for Greg to take these girls seriously dressed in evening wear. The girl who stayed on the couch wore a bra two sizes too small. Her nipples peeked over the edge of the white lace.

"Where's Lesley?"

"Who?"

"I mean, Porsche." He always forgot to call his sister by her stage name or whatever they called it.

"Oh, Porsche is in with a client." She walked behind the little counter where a day timer sat open under a tiny lamp. "Would you like to book an appointment?"

Two days ago, Lesley almost killed herself because she couldn't escape this life or her fear of Barry Ashford. But because of that fear, she was back, taking customers and reliving the horror that almost killed her. Greg wanted to burn the entire building to the ground. This woman asking if he wanted an appointment with his sister made it even worse.

"I do not want an appointment." He tried to stay in control. Every second his sister was in the other room was another second he had lost her.

The girl on the couch got up and rummaged in her purse for something.

"Stop the appointment and ask *Porsche* to come out here. I'm taking her home."

"And you are?" the tall one asked.

The girl with the half-exposed nipples finished rummaging in her purse and stood beside him.

"I'm her brother, and her name is Lesley, not Porsche."

The girls exchanged a look.

"Go get her," Greg ordered.

A door opened to the right. A tall man, well-built with thick arms, stepped out of a bathroom.

"There a problem here, ladies?" he asked.

Security.

"No, no problem," Greg said, his anger quelling any intimidation. "I'm just here to pick up my sister. Once she's in my car, I will leave peacefully."

The brick house of a man moved closer and looked down his nose at Greg. He had to be at least six-foot-seven, maybe taller.

"What if she isn't in your car when you leave?" He shrugged. "What then?"

Anger made men stupid. Greg knew it but didn't listen to the little man with a halo, dressed in white, perched on his shoulder, telling him to back up and come at this a different way. Instead, he moved closer to the man in front of him.

"If she isn't removed from her appointment and brought out to my car, I will burn this fucking place down, and I will make sure you're still in it." He stepped even closer, his nose almost touching the man's nose. "Back up out of my face."

"Or what?"

Greg was tired of the pissing contest. His knee came up so fast and hard that no one saw it in time. The air wheezed out of the security man's lungs as his eyes widened. He dropped to his knees, holding his crotch with both hands. As tall as he was, even at this angle, Greg was still nose to nose with him, although Greg was a little higher now.

He brought his knee up again, connecting with the man's chin. When he fell over, it rattled the floor.

When Greg turned to ask the tall whore to go and fetch his sister, the one with the exposed nipples had a small canister in her hand.

Liquid shot out of it, heading straight for Greg's face from six feet away. He ducked and spun on his heels as fast as he could. The canister's contents hit the back of his head as the girl screamed and unleashed another torrent of spray.

He would be blinded and hacking out a lung if he didn't get away from her. The only way out was the front door which was right in front of him.

He smacked into the door, ramming it open to get outside. As soon as the afternoon sun hit him, he ran for the end of the parking lot, where he crossed the street and headed to his car a block down.

He would return in an hour, and when he did, no one would stop him from taking Lesley.

No one at all because he would come with a gun.

He would be more prepared the next time.

Chapter 13

SARAH'S EYES FLUTTERED OPEN. She gasped, took a deep breath, and rolled away from the tree. She spread out on the carpet of pine needles, making sure nothing was damaged or broken. She had no way of knowing how long she had been out.

She pulled off her helmet and let it roll away. She would probably have a dented head if it hadn't been for the helmet.

A car approached on the road, passed her location, and faded away. At the top edge of the hill, where the grass stopped and the road began, a sign with an arrow warned drivers of the turn ahead. Since no emergency vehicles were in sight, she assumed no one had seen the accident. She assumed Barry didn't call it in.

That meant Barry had forced her off the road and then left without checking on her. He had meant to kill her. He must feel invincible. If Barry thought nothing could touch him, he had another thing coming.

Still looking skyward, she eased her phone out of her pocket, hoping it hadn't broken. Two in the afternoon. She had just over an hour to get to the Garden of Eden parlor at 3:17 p.m.

She brought the GPS tracker up on the screen. Barry's car was coming along McKinley Road, heading toward Glenmore, five minutes away.

After a couple of deep breaths, Sarah sat up, then got to her feet. No pain anywhere. Not even her head, where she had sustained a bullet wound only a few months ago.

Up a forty-five-degree embankment, the road had to be at least twenty feet away. The front wheel of her bike was twisted at an odd angle. She wasn't about to try to push it up the hill and drive it.

But how did she fly off the road and land down here with nothing even aching? It had to be Vivian. She knocked Sarah out like she had done before because a limp body—like extremely drunk—could fall from a five-story window of an apartment building, get up and walk away. Vivian had to have been involved.

She looked skyward again and blew a kiss into the air.

"I love you, Sis."

Sarah climbed, leaving the bike and helmet behind. At the road's edge, she ran toward the houses about five hundred yards down.

The tracker said that Barry's car was on Glenmore now and heading toward Union. He was three minutes away.

She picked up her speed. She had to meet him when she was ready, and as soon as she got the Jeep at Enterprise, she would go to the hardware store and be ready for the next time she saw Barry, which she suspected would be at 3:17 p.m.

Barry had turned onto Union. He would come into view in less than a minute. That wasn't enough time to reach the shelter of the houses.

Since she had started for the row of buildings along this road, not a single car had passed. On the other side of the road, just past the gravel shoulder, it dropped off, similar to where she had left her bike.

It was her only chance.

She ran across and jumped over the edge. It was steeper here. She slid to the bottom on her butt, then got to her feet. The ground leveled out fifteen feet below the edge of the road. A cover of pine trees hid her from view.

Just as she leaned on one of the trees to catch her breath, she heard his car. The tracker on her cell phone showed Barry's location almost right on top of her. From where she stood, back from the road, she had a clear view of the area where he had forced her into the ditch. Barry's car stopped there. He got out and walked to the edge of the shoulder to look down at Sarah's bike. Seeing she wasn't there, he scanned along the road both ways and scratched his head.

He grabbed for something in his jacket. A cell phone. He held it in front of him to see who was calling and then tapped a button.

He talked for a minute. His body language conveyed frustration and anger as he waved his free hand back and forth. He shouted something into the phone, ran around the car, and hopped in. A moment later, he squealed the tires as he took off.

She edged behind the tree as he passed her location, even though it would be hard for him to see her from the road while inside his car.

When the sound of his engine faded in the distance, she crawled back up to the road and continued toward the houses.

At the first one, she called Enterprise back on her cell phone.

"You still have that Jeep on hold for me?" she asked.

"Is this Sarah?"

"Yes."

"It's here."

"Would 3124 Sexsmith Road be inside your pickup zone?"

"Let me check." There was a moment of silence when she was put on hold. The afternoon sun beat down on her relentlessly. She wiped the sweat from her brow and remembered that she'd left the ball cap with the bike. "Sure, we'll come to pick you up there. I'll leave right now."

"Great. See you soon." She ended the call and started back for her bike.

She needed the ball cap, and she needed to have her hair tied up under it.

With her face all over the news and every cop in Kelowna looking for her, she needed to stay hidden in plain sight.

There were things to do and people to hurt.

And Sarah was pissed.

Her phone vibrated. She looked down at it.

Aaron. Oh, baby ...

She didn't answer it. When she could, she would call him back. Now wasn't the time.

He was supposed to let her have her space until she was ready to come back and face him.

She wondered what had changed, what made him call.

When she got to her bike and donned the hat, thoughts of Aaron left her mind. All she could think of was Barry Ashford. She needed to take this to another level. Wasn't she supposed to antagonize him until she found out his secrets? All the stuff Vivian still hadn't told her?

She was starting to like her new job.

The Antagonizer might even work as a new name.

She crawled back up the embankment and went to meet the car rental employee with less than an hour to go before she would enter the Garden of Eden Massage Parlor.

"I'm coming, Barry."

Chapter 14

THE BIKE WAS EXACTLY where it was supposed to be, but Sarah was gone. Only her helmet remained.

Barry checked the road but saw no sign of her.

Where the hell could she go?

His phone rang. He yanked it out.

The Garden of Eden.

"What's up?"

"Trouble," Nate said.

"Trouble? What kind of trouble?"

"Lesley's brother was just here."

"And?"

"He wanted to take Lesley with him. He hassled Rebecca and Julie at the front until I came out. Then he kneed me in the balls."

"He what!" Barry shouted. "How did he do that?"

"I didn't see it coming. Julie pepper-sprayed him, but he

ran outside and disappeared. He may come back."

Barry ran a hand through his hair. He had to fix this fast.

"Okay. I'm on my way. Don't do anything else. Keep Lesley there no matter what. If you have to lock the doors and shut the fucking place down, keep her there." He ran around his car and dropped in the front seat. "And watch the front doors. Don't let Greg in again. Got it?"

"Yeah."

"I'll make some calls. I'll take care of Greg."

"Good. And when you do, I want a shot at him. My fucking sac is bruised, man."

"Don't worry. You'll get yours."

He threw the phone onto the passenger seat and smacked the accelerator to the floor, fishtailing off the shoulder as he squealed away.

After a kilometer, he grabbed his phone and called Colin, who answered immediately.

"Yeah, Barry. What do you need?"

"You know a company called ReadyMaid Cleaners?"

"Yeah, weren't they the company suspected of all those break-ins a while ago?"

"That's them. I have proof that they were responsible for all those break-ins. But the proof is in their offices off Rutland Road. And the owner, Greg Wright, just assaulted Nate at the Garden."

"You looking for a warrant? Because if you are, I'm the wrong guy to call for that—"

"No, I just want Greg Wright, the owner of ReadyMaid, picked up. Can you run over to their offices and grab him, or go to his house?"

"You can't?"

"No. He just walked into the Garden of Eden and kicked Nate in the balls. I'm heading there now, but he got away. I think he knows I'm looking for him. All this time, and I never let it go. I've always believed Greg was responsible for those break-ins. Greg has harassed me before, keeping it legal but going at me just the same."

"Wow, you're going for a record this week."

"What do you mean?" Barry asked as he navigated the turn onto Harvey Avenue. Mid-afternoon traffic had thickened, and he had to make a sharper turn to avoid hitting a Hummer pulling a long trailer.

"First, the strange girl, and now Greg Wright."

"Maybe they're related," was all Barry could say.

"Possibly. Anyway, fine. I'll head out right now. It'll give me something to do."

"You're a pal."

Barry hung up and hit the gas. He would be at the Garden of Eden in less than five minutes. He would have a talk with Lesley in front of the other girls about having friends or relatives show up at her workplace. It was not good for business, and he wouldn't tolerate it. Once Lesley apologized to Rebecca and Julie and gave Nate a nice blow-job on his wounded prick, Barry would allow Lesley to shoot up directly. There would be no flash-blooding for her today. This incident was all the more reason for her to off herself. All Greg had done was add more proof that Lesley wanted to die by causing a disturbance. It would make her feel humiliated and embarrassed.

Before the evening's light fled the sky, Lesley would have overdosed in a back room, all by herself, filled with his seed. Her brother would be locked up downtown and arrested on assault charges.

Today was still going to turn out to be a glorious day.

He smiled at himself in the rearview mirror.

He was beautiful, and he knew it.

Chapter 15

The Enterprise Car Rental employee showed up fifteen minutes after Sarah had called. The driver picked her up and drove her to the office where Sarah had just finished with the paperwork.

She checked her phone. It was almost three in the afternoon. Then she checked the tracker on Barry's unmarked cruiser. It was parked at the Garden of Eden Massage Parlor.

Exactly where I'm heading.

"Okay," the clerk said. "Let's walk around the vehicle, and then you're set to go."

She had to assume he hadn't seen her picture in the news and didn't know the police were looking for her. The entire time she was in his presence, the clerk acted normal. He hadn't taken a second look at her or acted awkward in any way.

After the walk around, he handed her the keys, and Sarah

tore out of the parking lot with fifteen minutes to spare. Up the street, she pulled into a Canadian Tire store, where she bought a baseball bat and thick plastic ties.

Back in the Jeep, the dash clock read 3:14 p.m.

She wouldn't make it in three minutes.

"Shit!" she shouted in the front seat of the Jeep. "Please don't be a murder I'm supposed to stop."

She squealed out of the Canadian Tire parking lot, careful not to go more than ten kilometers over the speed limit.

Getting pulled over this close to the prophesied time would be a tragedy.

And Sarah hated to be late.

Chapter 16

Barry pulled up to the front entrance of the Garden of Eden, double-parked, and ran inside.

"What happened?" Barry asked.

Rebecca and Julie were on the couch watching TV. They looked calm and relaxed as if waiting for a customer.

Rebecca spoke first. "Lesley's brother"—she rolled a finger in a circle by her temple—"is a crazy mofo. Fucker comes in here demanding Lesley leave with him. Like, doesn't he know who be running this place?" She pointed her finger at him.

Both girls were chewing gum. Most of the girls chewed gum to get rid of the last customer's taste. Barry had considered bringing in a gum dispensing machine but eventually changed his mind. He made enough money off the girls that he didn't need to nickel and dime them their gum chewing.

"That's it?" Barry asked. "He demanded Lesley leave with him, and then he walked out when she didn't go?"

"He hit Nate, too. Ever since Nate's been watching for him. He just takes frequent bathroom runs to check his balls." Rebecca giggled.

This wasn't a time to giggle. He wanted to walk across the carpet and backhand that smile off her gum-chewing dirty mouth but restrained himself for now. He would hurt Rebecca the next time he brought her into his office for a heroin fix.

Nate stepped out of the bathroom.

"Tell me what happened," Barry said. "I want to know everything."

Nate shrugged as if it was no big deal. "Didn't expect him to knee me. Guess I need to be more alert."

"Has he come back? Have you seen him since he ran out?"

Nate shook his head. "Nope."

"Okay, if you do, call me right away. Every RCMP officer in Kelowna is looking for him as we speak. Not only did he assault you, but it looks like he's tied to a series of break-ins around Kelowna. Greg Wright is going down." He pulled his sleeve back and checked his watch. "It's just after three. Where's Lesley now?"

"In the back kitchen," Rebecca offered. "She's cool. No one told her about Greg's little visit. Her last customer just left."

He smiled. "Good thinking. Why tell her? It would only upset her and ruin her ability to make good money today." He moved around the counter and looked at the appointment book. "She has no one else scheduled for this afternoon?"

"Only Julie has an appointment. That crazy hockey player. But that's not for another half an hour. The rest of us are waiting around for walk-ins."

"Okay, here's what's going to happen. Lesley and I are going to have a *talk*. Then she's going for a smack ride to calm her down after I tell her what her brother did. No one is to disturb us. We will take the last room at the end of the hall. Understood? I mean, no one comes in for nothing. Even if Greg comes back," he turned to Nate, "you deal with it. Take the man down. Then drag him outside and call the police. But no one comes into the room Lesley and I are in. Cool?"

Rebecca was already looking back at the TV. She nodded. As far as Barry could tell, Julie hadn't heard a word he'd said.

"Can you handle Greg if he comes in?" Barry said as he tapped Nate's chest with a finger. "Call the cops. I don't want to be disturbed for at least an hour. Are we clear?"

Nate smiled as if he had caught on to what Barry had in mind. The one-on-one was always the hardest lesson for the girls. They're all required to participate in flash-blooding, or they don't make it a week at the Garden of Eden. Their side of the deal was they got free heroin, and sometimes Barry paid them for their personal attention to him. But one-on-one sessions were always brutal. Only a few girls had one-on-one sessions, and none could walk straight for a week afterward. They usually quit after those meetings. Maxine Freeman was the last girl in the Garden of Eden to have a one-on-one with Barry.

Lesley Wright wouldn't have the chance to quit. She was suicidal, and wasn't it convenient that her brother entered her place of employment today, attacked her coworkers, and made a scene, only to be arrested later in the day? Of course, it would be too much for Lesley to handle. No wonder she took that amount of heroin in the back room after her last customer.

Life can be hard for these stupid whores.

"I can handle it, boss. No one will disturb you." Nate patted Barry on the shoulder. "Go talk to Lesley. Straighten her out. Doesn't she need to make things good with the boss man?" He smiled at Barry as if he was in on some big conspiracy.

Barry headed toward the back of the building, already feeling his erection coming to life. At the kitchen door, he spotted her at the table, a cookie in her hand, crumbs on her lips.

"How are you feeling?" he asked.

When she looked up, her eyes were bloodshot with bags under them. Normally he would chastise her for looking like shit, remind her to keep her weight down and send her home. But today, he had other uses for her.

At least no other customers would have to be exposed to her. Ever again.

"I'm okay," Lesley said, her voice sad and forlorn.

"We need to talk, Lesley. Please come into room four."

She pushed her plastic container of cookies away and got up. He stepped into room four and waited for her to follow. Once inside, he locked the door and pocketed the key.

The room was the same as the others, complete with a shower and a massage table that doubled as a bed.

"Take your clothes off and get on the bed."

Lesley turned around, tears in her eyes. "Barry, I'm sorry. I won't try to kill myself again. I don't even know why I jumped from that bridge." She moved closer and touched his arm. "I'll be good. Just give me a chance."

He pulled out a needle. "All you need is a little more relaxation."

"No, no, please, that's why I jumped in the first place. No more smack. Please. I can't handle the thought of sharing blood anymore." Frantic, she rubbed his arm as she pleaded for him to understand. "Who knows what diseases we're spreading around? I just can't do it anymore."

Without warning, he backhanded Lesley. All the pent-up anger of the past few days channeled through his hand. She dropped to the floor like a discarded doll. Her moans quickly turned into a scream.

He kicked her in the stomach with the toe of his boot. "Shut your fucking mouth."

He dropped the needle back in his pocket, grabbed her arms, and dragged her to the bed. After helping her up onto it, he leaned in close to her face. Blood spilled from the side of her mouth.

"Scream, protest, or try to escape, and I will kill you," he whispered. "Got that?"

He pulled the needle out and then produced an arm strap from his other pocket. She rolled away from him and faced the wall, sobbing. He set her arm up and prepared to inject the heroin into a vein that was clearly ready.

Once she was under, getting her clothes off would be hard and take longer than he wanted.

"Remove what you are wearing before we get started."

Reluctantly, Lesley did as she was told. It didn't take long as she only wore a bra, panties, and a small negligee. Now naked on the bed but for the strap around her arm, he shot the first dose into her vein and waited a few seconds until she was under its spell.

He got the needle ready to go again, but first, he wanted his fun with her. After all the trouble she had caused, he deserved this. She owed him. It was her fault Greg came running in earlier. It was probably her fault that that stupid girl was harassing him. Everything was Lesley's fault. A little payback was due.

He rolled her onto her stomach. She smiled and writhed with the effects of the drug.

The lubricant was on the table. He grabbed it and poured a liberal amount onto her buttocks. Then he rubbed it between them and smeared it on her anus.

She was ready to receive him. No condom. No easing her into it. No nothing. This was her last fuck, and he would do it his way.

After taking his shirt and pants off, he stood in his underwear, his member rock-hard in anticipation. Then he prepared the needle for one more large dosage into her other arm.

There was a commotion at the front of the parlor.

Who could that be?

It was probably Greg. He would have returned, and Nate was dealing with it. That's why he'd hired Nate.

Footsteps pounded down the hall. It didn't faze Barry. No one could get in with the door locked.

He undid the strap and applied it to the other arm.

"You doing okay, Lesley?" He ran a finger through her cheeks and squeezed it inside her anus. "We're going to get a little higher, and then I'm going to place things in here. Is that okay with you?"

She moaned.

"I thought so."

He withdrew his finger and set the needle to her vein.

"Here we go."

Chapter 17

SARAH PULLED INTO THE parking lot five minutes past the time Vivian told her to be there. Fearful of what she might have missed, she almost jumped out of the Jeep before it stopped moving.

She grabbed the baseball bat and jammed the twist ties into her back pocket. With a quick swing of her arm, the Jeep door slammed shut.

"Hey!" someone yelled to her left.

She dropped close to the ground and spun toward the voice, the bat raised over her shoulder.

Greg Wright?

She lowered the bat and straightened up. "Greg? What are you doing here?"

He looked harried, his eyes wild as he bounced on the balls of his feet.

"I came earlier, and they wouldn't let me take my sister."

"She's back already? After what happened a few days ago?"

He nodded. "And I know for a fact that she doesn't want to be here." He looked down at the bat. "What's that for?"

"Anyone who gets in my way. Let's get Lesley out together. Follow me."

Sarah hid the bat behind her right leg and headed along the side of the building to the front door. Without knowing for sure why she had to be here, Sarah had to assume it was for Barry. His car was parked out front, and it hadn't moved since she tracked it on her cell phone.

Officer Ashford had to be her target. He ran her off the road. Cop or no cop, he was running a massage parlor and doing something called flash-blooding. He was also holding Lesley Wright against her will.

The carpet in her basement was pulled back. The chair was in place. Even the camera was aimed at the chair. With Sarah's basement ready for interrogation, it was time to abduct Officer Ashford and lock him up in her cellar. Sarah would take Barry out, and Greg could take his sister.

Anyone who tried to stop them would have to deal with her friend, the aluminum bat.

She opened the front doors and walked in. Greg stayed outside for some reason, fidgeting with his pants.

Two girls sat on a couch. They both stared at her, then glanced at the bat. A large man stood beside the couch, leaning against the wall. He looked past her at Greg. His eyes widened, and his mouth formed a circle.

"Where's Barry Ashford?" Sarah asked. She jerked her head back in a quick motion at Greg. "And where's his sister?"

Both girls checked her out. They looked her up and down as if she was applying for a job. She raised the bat and brought it down in the center on the small counter to her left to get their attention. The counter cracked, and the lamp bounced and fell over. One of the girls let out a small scream.

Barry would probably be armed. A quick glance down the hallway confirmed it was still empty.

"Answer the lady," Greg said from behind her.

She turned to look at Greg. He held a Smith and Wesson in his shaking hands.

"What's that for?" she asked.

"Anyone who gets in my way. I'm leaving with my sister."

"Well, that changes things." Sarah lowered the bat and moved closer to the tall man. Both girls sank deeper into the sofa at the sight of Greg's gun.

"Where's Barry Ashford and Greg's sister?"

When no one answered her, Sarah turned to Greg, "Shoot this one first." She pointed at the large man. When his attention was on Greg, she swung the bat sideways and whacked the side of his right knee. He grunted and crumpled to the floor, curling into a ball. Teeth squeezed tight, lips back, he breathed in and out through his mouth as his face turned beet red.

Sarah rested the bat on her shoulder and looked down at the two girls on the sofa.

"He might not," she gestured at Greg, "but I hit girls. Either one of you want to spend a week in the hospital, or would you rather tell me where Barry and Lesley are?"

The brunette pointed down the hall. "Room four. The door will be locked. He told us not to let anyone disturb him."

"Perfect." She turned to Greg. "Let's go disturb him."

She ran down the hall and tried the knob.

Locked.

To break the lock with the bat would take too long.

She whispered to Greg. "Shoot into the knob here. But angle it down so you don't hit anyone who might be close to the door. With your nerves, it might take a few tries."

Greg got into position after Sarah walked around behind him.

The sound of the gun firing in the small hallway was deafening. Greg pulled the trigger three times, then jumped sideways and body-checked the door.

It flew inward on its hinges and smacked the wall, with Greg almost losing his balance as he stumbled inside. He smacked into a table and dropped the gun. Sarah was close behind, her bat up and ready.

When Sarah took in the sight, she was happy that the gun was still not in Greg's hand. Otherwise, he probably would've shot Barry where he stood.

Barry was in his underwear, holding Lesley's arm, a needle protruding from her flesh. She was naked, lying on her stomach with something shiny plastered all over her rear end.

What had Barry been doing to her? Or had they arrived in time because he was still in his underwear?

"Step away from her," Sarah said.

"And what if I don't?"

Greg collected himself. The gun was still on the floor, near the base of the small table.

"I will murder you with my bare hands," Greg managed

to say, "if you have done anything to my sister."

"What? Like this?"

He plunged the needle into Lesley's arm.

"NO!" Greg yelled and dove at Barry.

It looked like the needle was fully plunged before Greg tackled Barry to the floor.

Lesley writhed on the bed in the throes of the drug.

Sarah reached down and retrieved the gun. She leveled it and fired toward the base of the shower. The stall's glass door shattered in an ear-splitting cadence. Both men stopped grappling on the floor and looked at her.

"Get up, or I will shoot you in the forehead."

Barry scrambled to his feet.

"Greg, your sister needs you. Wrap something around her and put her in your car. Get her to the nearest hospital fast, or you might lose her."

Greg punched Barry in the face. Then he rolled away, grabbed the negligee on the floor, and wrapped it around Lesley, who started to shake on the table. He lifted her off the bed, his strong arms flexing as if he curled women at the gym all the time.

He ran by Sarah and said, "Thanks."

Sarah pulled the twist ties from her pocket and tossed them at Barry. They landed at his bare feet. "Put one of these on your wrists."

"I'm an officer of the law. A member of the Royal Canadian Mounted Police force, and you are—"

She turned slightly and fired into the baseboard behind his leg. He jumped like a startled cat.

"That was the last warning shot," she said. "The next one opens you up. Now tie your wrists or test me again."

With a hand on the bed, he got to his feet. He leaned over and picked up the ties. After fumbling with one of them for a second, he managed to get it around his wrists but couldn't find the right angle to tighten it.

Sarah reached in and grabbed the exposed length, and pulled. The tie slid tight, locking his wrists together. With the gun pressing into the naked flesh of his stomach, she bent down and grabbed his shirt.

"Turn around."

Once his back was to her, she draped the shirt over his head and tied the arms together around his neck as best as she could. It was tight enough to stay on his head but not tight enough to strangle him.

"Follow my lead. Fuck around, and I'll shoot you. Got it."

He nodded.

With the gun in her right hand, she guided him out of the room with her left. They walked up the hallway unobstructed. In the front foyer, the two girls were gone. The big man she had whacked with the baseball bat was still on the floor. She might have hit him harder than she thought, and now he had trouble walking.

"Nate?" Barry said from under his shirt. "Hey, Nate, you there?"

The big guy on the floor didn't respond.

Sarah nudged Barry to keep going. They continued for the door. As she got there, an aging thin man with gray hair opened it. He stopped to let Sarah and Barry exit.

The guy frowned when he saw Barry in his underwear with a shirt wrapped around his head. Then his eyes lit up on the gun jammed into Barry's side.

"Fetish thing," Sarah said. "Got to keep it as real as possible." She smiled at the man holding the door as she walked by him.

He shrugged. "Whatever floats your boat."

"She's lying," Barry said. "Help me."

Sarah shrugged back at the man by the door. "Authentic, eh?"

The man walked inside and closed the door behind him.

"Come on, asshole." Sarah pushed Barry to walk faster.

"Ouch," he said as his bare feet stumbled along the pavement. "What are you doing? Kidnapping me?"

She popped the tailgate. "Get in." She shoved him hard.

He banged his head and dropped to the Jeep floor, where he curled up and moaned, covering the side of his head with his bound hands.

Sarah shut the back door and ran around to the front seat. Before starting the Jeep, she saw the two girls from the couch. They were standing at the edge of the parking lot. They were probably waiting for the police but had decided to wait outside since Greg had come in packing a gun.

It looked like the blonde one smiled and nodded at Sarah.

They're probably happy someone is finally taking the garbage out.

"We're going for a little ride," Sarah said, loud enough for Barry to hear. "If you take that shirt off your head, I will kill you in the bush, use a saw to dismember your body, and leave you as dinner for the wildlife in the area. Are we clear?"

"Yes," was the mumbled reply.

Sarah started the Jeep and pulled out of the parking lot. She hoped Lesley was going to be okay. If Lesley didn't overdose, she would never have to worry about Barry Ashford again.

No one would have to worry about Barry Ashford ever again.

Sarah was sick and tired of men like Barry who did what they wanted and got away with it because they were part of the street gang in blue. The gang that wore badges. Sure, there were good cops, but bad ones were the only kind Sarah was interested in, and she had a live one in her Jeep.

All she had to do was hurt him until he broke and told her everything that Vivian had sent her to antagonize out of him.

Then maybe this task would be over. But Vivian had said Barry was the barnacle on a ship and that Sarah was here for something much darker.

What could be darker than raping drugged girls?

Chapter 18

Sarah arrived home without interruption. No one was searching for her in a brand-new Jeep. She backed into her driveway so the tailgate would open in privacy. The only neighbor was Barry's wife, Deborah, and Sarah didn't want to take any chances.

She turned the vehicle off and waited, listening to the engine ticking as it cooled.

"Where are we?" Barry asked.

"In fuck you land."

"Oh, I get it. You're not going to tell me?"

"No, I'm not going to tell you."

Sarah got out and looked at Ashford's house. Deborah's car wasn't in the driveway.

Maybe she parked it in the garage.

They had one room that extended to the edge of their property. This was the room Debbie had watched Sarah from the night she arrived to meet the landlords. It was the only room that could see Sarah's driveway clearly.

The drapes remained still. As far as Sarah could tell, no one stood in the window, peeking out.

At the front door to her house, she unlocked it and left it standing wide open. Then she ran back to the Jeep, popped the tailgate, and helped Barry out.

"Don't try to be a hero," she said. "I've still got the gun."

"Seriously? How do you expect to get away with this? You are kidnapping a member of the RCMP. Are you aware of the jail sentence attached to something like this?"

"I don't think about things like that. If I did, it would stop me in my tracks. I would end up living in a remote cabin, writing messages on the walls and repainting over them again and again. If I worried about the authorities, I'd lose my sanity."

She pushed him through the front door and slammed it shut behind her. With a firm grip on his arm, she led him toward the stairs.

"Where are we going?" he asked.

She didn't answer. At the top of the stairs, she turned to him.

"Stairs," she instructed. "Going down. Take one at a time."

He tried to turn around, his bound hands flailing for the wall. "No, I can't go in a basement."

"Why not?"

"I hate basements. I just don't do basements."

She put a hand on his chest. "You're going down on your feet or your ass. After what I caught you doing to Lesley, do you think I care whether you like basements? Now turn around and walk, or I will shove you down."

He rested his forehead against the wall. "Please. Don't."

"Down. Now."

He turned slowly, tested the step with his toes, and moved down one. Then another. The going was slow, but at least he was going.

Three steps from the bottom, visibly shaking, he stopped and placed his right shoulder against the wall.

"I can't. I just can't go any farther."

Sarah slipped Greg's gun into the back of her pants. Open-palmed, she shoved Barry off the third step. He was low enough to miss clipping his head on the slanted roof but couldn't stay on his feet. He dropped the last three steps and sprawled on the floor.

Barry Ashford was always in charge. He wore the badge. No one ever touched him inappropriately. Because of that, Sarah needed to break him. She needed to touch, prod, punch, and smack as much as possible.

"Hey, you don't want to do this," he yelled from the floor. He grabbed at the shirt tied around his neck, trying to loosen it.

Sarah let him. He was in her basement now, and his hands were still tied. She had the gun. It didn't matter if he could see now.

She pulled the gun out and aimed it at the floor. Barry fought with the shirt until it lifted above his eyes. Then it was off completely, and he lay on the floor, naked but for his underwear, nipples erect in response to the cold tiles.

His head swiveled around, taking in the basement. "Where are we?"

"Get on the chair." She pointed at the chair in the center

of the concrete floor.

When he looked back at her, his eyes were wide, rimmed in red. "You can't be serious. You're going to interrogate me?"

She tapped the gun with her free hand and extended her arm to aim it at him. "Listen to me when I talk and do what I say. Get in the chair."

While he hesitated, Sarah wondered if the sound of the gun going off would attract anyone. Since Deborah was the closest neighbor, and her car wasn't in the driveway, there was a high chance no one would hear the gun. But what if she was home and her car was just in the garage? Would she hear it and call the police?

Sarah squeezed her trigger finger, still debating if this was a good idea.

Barry decided for her. He moved, edging along the floor toward the chair. Once in the chair, he sat facing her.

"Now what?" he asked.

"Use the duct tape. Wrap your ankles to the front legs of the chair." She walked across the basement and leaned against the wall at least seven feet from him. She would get a shot off from this distance before he could tackle her if he tried. "No protesting. Just do it."

He grabbed the tape easily as his hands were tied in front and began securing himself to the chair.

"I was saying earlier how much trouble this could lead to." He bit the end of the tape and tore it, wrapping the rest around his right ankle. Then he started on the left. "So why are you doing this? The trouble you're in will be unavoidable. You will never recover." He did three circles around his left ankle, bit the tape, and finished. It looked like a pretty good job considering his hands were tied. He sat up straight and glared at her, his face red from the exertion. "You're not going to kill me. We both know that. Nobody kidnaps and kills cops. So why are you doing this? What's it all for? What's your end game?"

She pushed off the wall and approached him. When she put her hand out, he placed the tape in it. After securing the gun back in her pants, she pulled out a long strip of tape and attached it to his chest. Then, going in circles around him, she strapped him to the chair, immobilizing him until someone came with scissors. Even the tops of his arms were locked down with his chest. He was now limited to the least amount of mobility.

"When you die," Sarah said, "the things you do for yourself die with you. But the things you do for others live on as your legacy."

"So you're doing this for someone else?" He shook his head in disgust and looked at the floor. "I can't believe that. No one is that selfless. Tell me something." He looked back up at her. "Who kidnaps an RCMP officer and ties him to a chair at gunpoint for someone else?"

"I do. My name is Sarah Roberts, and I do it for all the girls you've hurt and all the girls you were planning to hurt in the future. I do it for girls like Lesley Wright."

He coughed up phlegm and spit on the floor. "Fuck you, Sarah. You know nothing about me."

She stepped back and admired her handiwork. "If you yell, I will tape your mouth, and it won't be a single strip. I will wrap the tape around your head as I've done with your chest."

"Don't worry. I won't yell. I will sit here and enjoy our

time together. They'll find me eventually, and you will go to jail. People saw you take me out of the Garden of Eden." He laughed. "You're so stupid." He laughed again like this was all just one big party gag. "The police will be here within the hour. I'll be having dinner tonight at home while you're rotting in a holding cell until your arraignment in the morning." His arrogant smile irritated her. "So, tell me, what have you brought me down here to talk about?"

She flicked on the light. It shined in his face. The DVR would be recording as there was plenty of movement in front of the camera. She stepped into the storage room and grabbed a small handsaw, a wooden block, and a roll of paper towels.

When she came back out, his body glistened with sweat.

"You okay, Barry?"

"Yeah, just a little warm."

"It's cool in this basement." She offered a wry smile. "Or are you afraid of the basement?"

He blew air out of his lips. "Shit, I'm not afraid of them. I just hate basements."

She set the wooden block and the handsaw on a table and then pulled it over beside the chair.

"What are you doing?" he asked.

"We're going to play a game."

"What kind of game involves a handsaw?"

"A truth game." *Vivian, I hope you're right about this.*

"Interrogation?"

"Game sounds more fun." She gave him a crazy smile and blinked erratically, trying to look as insane as she could muster. "Doesn't it?"

Sweat dripped from his brow. "I have to take a piss. How am I expected to do that?"

"You don't."

"What?" He sounded shocked. "I have to piss. It's not something you just decide not to do."

"Piss in your underwear. Shit where you sit, for all I care. When our talk is over, and you've told me everything I want to know, I will untie you, and you'll be able to use the restroom. I'll even let you shower before the real police get here. Cool?"

"You're crazy. You can't do this—"

"Ahh, but I *am* doing it."

She held out her hand, her baby finger extended toward him.

"What's this?" he asked.

"Pinky swear."

"Are you crazy? What are we, in high school?"

She wrapped her pinky around his. "Now, pinky swear that you'll tell me the truth and nothing but the truth, and you will never break that promise to me. When I ask a question, you answer it. Got it?"

"I'm not going to pinky swear to anything—"

With her right hand free, she came around fast, formed a fist on the way, and sucker-punched Barry in the jaw. His head snapped to the side, straining the duct tape around his chest.

"What did you do that for?" he asked.

"You honor and respect me in my house, in my basement. There will be no talking back and no fucking around."

"You've lost your mind."

"Certifiable." She blinked twice, widened her eyes, and tilted her head. Then she slipped her pinky inside his again.

"Pinky swear you'll tell me the truth and answer every question or face the consequences."

"Okay, fine, whatever you want. I pinky swear."

"Perfect." Sarah pulled her hand away and moved to the side table with the wooden block and the handsaw. "When Greg and I walked into room number four at the Garden of Eden Massage Parlor today, you had Lesley naked on a massage table, bed, or whatever you call it. She had something shiny on her butt. What was that?"

"Lubrication."

"What for?"

He turned to look up at her. "You don't know what lube is for? You're a pretty girl. I'm sure you're not that stupid."

"What was in the needle in her arm?"

"Red Bull." He chuckled again. "We inject that shit, so the sex is extra good."

"Was she a willing partner?"

He didn't answer.

"I understand flash-blooding involves the sharing of the blood from someone high on heroin." His head snapped to look at her. "Since there was only the two of you, and your flash-blooding game involves more than one girl at a time, what were you doing to Lesley? Trying to rape her? Or were you assisting in her wish for suicide?"

"How do you know—" He swallowed. "Where did you hear about flash-blooding?"

"Raping her or killing her? Answer the question."

"What does it matter?" He turned away. "I'm done talking to you. Get out of my face. I'll just sit here like a good little boy until the police come."

"Wrong answer." She cuffed the back of his head. "One

more time. Raping her or trying to kill her? Last chance, and I don't bluff."

"Fuck you, Sarah."

An image of Aaron flashed into her mind. A physical ache drifted through her chest. She thought of Parkman and the times they'd had together. The image of him on his knees in front of her saying he would rather die than beg Sarah Roberts for his life because if he did, she wouldn't respect him anymore. Aaron and Parkman were real men. Barry Ashford was a piece of shit on the bottom of their shoes.

A cop was tied up in her basement. Without a real confession on tape, she would face ten years in prison for this. She had passed the point of no return without something earth-shattering to go on. There was no coming back from this, no recovery except for a full confession of everything Vivian had sent her to discover.

Desperate, alone, and angry, she was stunned into inaction. Was all this about drugs? Sex with girls who worked at a massage studio? If that were the case, hundreds, if not thousands, of men would need to be rounded up and arrested.

Sarah had gone too far this time, and she knew it. But Barry had also gone too far. He was about to rape Lesley when they stopped him. He was probably trying to kill her, too. Laws didn't punish the rapist as much as the tax evader. That sent the wrong message.

Since Sarah was young, she hated the police, even the sight of their uniforms. Rationally, she knew they weren't all bad. It was something she couldn't explain, something she couldn't change. But it was real.

And this rapist cop sitting in front of her was real. When

this was all over, the worst that would happen to him would be paid leave until his day in court, and anything on the DVR would be inadmissible as it was obtained under duress. In the end, Sarah would be arrested and jailed because she kidnapped him and caused the duress.

Her pulse quickened at the injustice of it all. She ground her teeth together, and a rage brewed as she stared at him. She wanted to hurt him for what he had been doing to all the women in The Garden of Eden.

She grabbed his bound hands, pulled them to the side, and then pressed them down onto the wooden block. Holding Barry's hands steady, bracing his forearms against her hip, she picked up the handsaw.

"Did you know that the pinky swear originally meant the person who broke the promise had to cut off their baby finger?" Sarah asked.

"What?" he yelled. "No!"

"You swore you would answer my questions and tell me the truth. You lied."

She applied the handsaw to his baby finger, added body weight to the pressure, and thought about Lesley, naked and about to be raped. She saw the cop touching her as a young girl, threatening her mother's life if she told anyone. Hatred for the violations men like Barry perpetrated on women made her hand move.

Sarah sliced back and forth across Barry's baby finger as he screamed.

And then he screamed some more.

Chapter 19

DEBORAH ASHFORD WAS PRETTY sure Sarah hadn't seen her in the window. Living at the end of such a quiet street, she could hear a car coming from a mile away. She always knew when Barry came home, just as she had known Sarah pulled up on her motorcycle that first night. But where was her bike now? Sarah was driving a new Jeep. Had she rented it? Why would she when she had a motorcycle? Deborah assumed the vehicle change was because the police were looking for Sarah.

The drapes had fallen back into place as Sarah pulled in next door. The slit between the drapes was wide enough to watch Sarah easily.

Sarah had opened the back of the Jeep and pulled out a man, naked but for his boxers, bound at the wrists and a shirt tied over his head. Deborah would recognize that body anywhere.

It was Barry Ashford, her husband.

Deborah stood on her carpeted guest room floor and stared through the slit in the curtains until long after Sarah had taken him into her house. What could have possibly transpired for that nice young girl, a writer visiting from the States, to abduct Barry and take him into her rental home? Joan and Mike would be quite upset when they found out.

Deborah eventually moved to the kitchen, making a cup of loose-leaf tea. She had to think. She was missing something. There had to be a reason for what Sarah was doing.

Barry had said something about Sarah harassing him. That was why the police were looking for her. But she seemed like such a nice girl. Why would she harass an RCMP officer? What could she possibly gain from it? Abducting him was very serious, and that scared Deborah. But there was something subtly attractive about it. What if Sarah hurt Barry? Or worse, killed him?

She smiled as she sipped her tea.

After all the years of abuse, the hitting, the punching, Deborah was happy that Barry was getting his. She knew what he did with those sluts at the massage parlor. Her heart had blackened years ago, with no chance of regaining its original vitality. She was too old to find another man. In the back of her mind, she always wondered if Barry would die in the line of duty. Being a cop was risky business. But nothing ever happened to Barry. He would come home drunk, smelling of other women's perfumes, and fall asleep. He would yell at her, hit her, and complain about how much money she had spent.

Sometimes, she wondered why she was even in Barry's

life. It was clear he wanted to live the life of a swinging bachelor. But what if she left? What would she ever amount to? Staying at home and making the best of it was all she had. There had been good times, but those were in the early days. Now she drank too much, spent too much money, and blamed everything on Barry.

Whatever Sarah was up to was fine. Deborah's face still ached from the last time Barry hit her. Maybe Sarah would hurt him. When he gets rescued eventually, maybe he would be humbled. He hadn't felt real pain in a long time. He dished it out often enough, but he never felt any. No one ever went after Barry; maybe that was why this was happening.

Perhaps he pissed off the wrong girl.

You just never knew who you were dealing with. Sarah could be connected to the underworld, where a cop's life was worthless. Or she could be an undercover FBI agent from the States and, during her investigation, had found out what Barry was doing at the massage parlor.

Deborah smiled again.

After all these years, Barry might just be getting his own medicine.

Her stomach twitched with excitement.

She moved to the living room where she would sip her tea, read her Jack Ketchum novel, *Off Season*, and wait for someone to come to the door. It would either be Barry coming home or Sarah coming over to ask her questions about her husband's activities.

Or it would be the police looking for her husband, in which case she would lie.

"No, Officer," Deborah said out loud. "I haven't seen Barry in days. I have no idea where my husband has gone, but he's done this before. Sorry I can't help you more."

Soon, she would learn the whole story, and she admitted to herself, guiltily, that it would please her to find out her husband got a little hurt in the process.

After all the beatings she had to endure over the years and the humiliation of being violated when he would come home drunk and covered in another woman's stench, she secretly hoped Barry was being tortured next door.

"You go, Sarah."

She sipped her tea, staring out the window at Okanagan Lake, her novel forgotten momentarily.

A plan began to form. She thought about it some more and then made a decision.

Her smile widened as she raised her mug to toast the air.

"Oh, how devious, Debbie, how devious you are. Barry won't even see it coming. Neither will Sarah."

Chapter 20

GREG PACED THE WAITING room floor, eager to hear anything about his sister's condition. A door opened on the side of the room, and the doctor emerged.

"How is she?" Greg asked.

The doctor's white coat was stained red in some places and a jaundiced yellow in others. It looked like he had personally attended to the victims of a bus accident at the scene of the crash. His glasses looked too thick for him to see properly, but Greg's sister was admitted for an overdose. Even though Greg's anxiety grew at the doctor's appearance, maybe the man was qualified enough to handle Lesley.

"She's going to make it," he said. "Close call with that much heroin in her system, but she'll pull through. You're going to have to consider an intervention and rehab after this. Her arms indicate this wasn't the first time."

Doors opened behind him. Greg turned around. Two

uniformed police officers and a man in a suit walked through and stopped behind him.

"I had to call them," the doctor said. "She was half-naked when she got here, and it appeared that she had been violated. These men will want your statement, and when Lesley wakes, they'll also want to speak to her."

Whatever they were going to do to him for taking a gun into the Garden of Eden was nothing now that Lesley was okay. He would get a lawyer and fight Barry Ashford. When it was all over, he would close up shop, grab Lesley and leave town. As far as he was concerned, the Wright family was done with Kelowna. They could keep their crime and their rogue cops.

"Mr. Wright. I'm Detective Colin Lang." He held out his ID. "Could you come with us?"

Greg turned back to the doctor. "If I'm not back by the time she's ready to be released, will you at least tell her to get in touch with me? Tell her to call her brother."

"I will, Mr. Wright." The doctor patted him on the shoulder.

Greg followed the officers through the hospital corridors until they got outside. One of the men opened the back door of an unmarked cruiser.

"Where are we going?" Greg asked.

"Get in."

Detective Lang's tone warned Greg not to ask any more questions. He got in the back and squished his legs against the steel barricade at the back of the front seat.

The uniformed officers got in beside him, and Lang drove away from the hospital. Were they bad cops taking him to a dumpster where they would kill him with a gun that had the serial number filed off?

Maybe I watch too much TV.

As they pulled in front of the police station off Ellis Street in downtown Kelowna, he realized he was only freaking himself out. They didn't cuff him, which he took as a good sign. He could handle this. For Lesley, he would get through it.

After escorting him inside, they led him down a long corridor to a series of doors, where they opened one and gestured for him to go in.

A metal table and two chairs. Classic interrogation room.

The officer shut the door, leaving him alone.

He sat and waited. It gave him time to think about how he would get out of this mess. What Barry had been about to do to his sister was horrific. Going in with a gun and pulling Lesley out of there couldn't get him in too much trouble unless it turned into his word against Barry's.

But what about Sarah? He had left her there. Where was she now? Where was Barry?

Before Detective Lang entered the small room to talk to him, Greg had already decided to say nothing until he had a lawyer present. The chance of saying something wrong and incriminating Sarah terrified him. After all that she had done by putting Lesley first, he just wouldn't do it.

He had time. Lesley was at the hospital recuperating. There was nothing to gain by cooperating right away and getting released. He could relax, get his head together and talk through a lawyer.

Lang entered slowly, closed the door, and sat across from Greg.

"Can I get you tea? A coffee?"

Greg shook his head. It made him nervous about defying the police. But he reminded himself that it was his right to have counsel present.

A thought struck him: *no one had read me my rights.*

"Do you need a bathroom?" Lang asked.

Greg shook his head again.

"Then we'll begin."

"Lawyer first."

The detective glanced up at him. "You haven't been charged with anything. Are you sure you want to lawyer up? I just want to talk."

"If you just want to talk, take me to a local bar. Buy me a drink. We'll talk. Bring me down here like you did, then I want a lawyer." He spoke fast before he changed his mind.

"Fair enough."

Lang moved for the door.

"Before long, I'll have someone bring a phone in."

"Phone book too."

"You don't have a lawyer?"

"There's some in the phone book. I'll have one soon enough."

Lang stepped into the corridor and shut the door.

Chapter 21

SARAH STOOD BACK AGAINST the wall and took in the scene. She let the handsaw drop from her fingers. It clattered to the floor by her feet.

Barry had stopped screaming. He whimpered softly, his chin resting on his chest.

Blood covered the wooden block. A considerable amount of blood had spilled on the floor, but not enough to be life-threatening. What was left of his baby finger was on the floor. She wasn't going to ice it. They wouldn't reattach it. Barry would have to live the rest of his life with nine digits and a stump. It would serve as a reminder of what he had done to Lesley and all the girls before her.

Sarah wrapped the stump in gauze with a wad of paper towels around that. His hand was buried in a mound of a white towel, stained red.

Not on any level did she take pleasure from what she had

done. But when she saw Barry in that room, drugging Lesley, probably enough to kill her just so he could perform his demented debauchery on her, something changed in Sarah. Castration came to mind. She wanted to cut him badly, hurt him, and make him bleed. He was a cop. He was supposed to protect and serve. Instead, he was abusing his position in the most grotesque way.

Just like the cop who used to babysit Sarah when she wasn't even a teenager yet.

If Barry didn't tell her what she wanted to know, if he didn't open up and tell her everything Vivian had sent her here to find out, she would do much worse than removing one small finger.

She pushed off the wall and went upstairs without a word. He didn't say anything as she left. He just kept whimpering, his head bowed.

At the front window, she checked outside. Nothing was amiss. No cop cars, no visitors, no Deborah.

At the back of the house, she looked through all the windows.

Nothing.

The police would be involved by now. Nate or those two girls would've called. They would've grabbed Greg at the hospital when he took Lesley in. But no one knew where Sarah lived. The house was in the landlord's name. The phone, the internet, and even the electricity bill all came in their name. The only thing linking Sarah to the outside world was the car rental. But there was no Enterprise Rental Car sticker on it.

She had to assume that a description of the Jeep would be circulated by the end of the day.

Her time in the Jeep was limited. She needed to get enough food to last a couple of days before everyone and their neighbor were looking for her vehicle.

But before that, talking to Barry while he was reeling from the loss of his finger might produce the results she wanted.

She grabbed a glass of water when all the lights were off and headed back downstairs. She wanted to stay hydrated for the long night ahead.

She pulled a chair out of storage and sat down behind the bright light that shone on Barry, keeping herself off-camera in the dark.

"Talk," she said. "Tell me about your life. Tell me all the bad things you've been up to. List it all. I want names, dates, and places. Everything you can think of. When you're done, and I'm satisfied, I will untie you and allow you to leave. You can see to that finger of yours. Get it properly dressed." She sipped from her water. "If you tell the truth, there will be no more violence. I don't bluff. If I say you can go, I mean it. So talk."

There was enough play in his bound wrists to hold the paper towels tight around his bleeding finger to staunch the flow.

"Talk," Sarah said again. "Do it now. I won't keep asking."

"There's nothing …" he said, pain straining his voice. "Nothing to say."

"Oh. Okay. I see. Which finger gets lopped off next?" She leaned forward in her chair. "When I'm done with fingers, maybe I will castrate you. A man can live without a penis, you know. Women have been doing it for years."

His face was blanched, red orbs for eyes. "Why are you doing this?"

"Any of your victims ask you that before you abused them?"

A tear crept down his cheek. "Is that what this is all about?"

"You tell me. Talk about your life. List all your indiscretions. I want to know everything."

"Would you like me to repent? Say I'm sorry? I can't go back and fix what I've done. On the outside, it looks bad, but some of those girls liked it. Some loved it."

"You're delusional. Keep talking like that, and I'll stop cutting fingers off. I'll just cut both of your hands off instead. Let's see how many more women you rape with no *fucking* hands."

"Some even asked me for more," he pleaded.

"That's their drug addiction talking. You get them addicted so that they will beg you for more. Eases your conscience, doesn't it?"

He looked at the ceiling, shook his head, then lowered it.

"Roll your eyes. Shake your head." She ground her teeth. "Continue to be disrespectful, and I will hurt you so bad you'll be begging me to paralyze you so you won't feel the pain your lower body will be dealing with."

He raised his head but looked to the side, avoiding her gaze. "Okay, I'll talk."

"Tell me about flash-blooding."

"I went to Africa a few years ago. I learned about it there. A cost-effective way for more than one person to get high on only one stash of heroin." He licked his lips. "Do you think I could get a drink?"

"No. Keep talking."

"After injecting the heroin in the first person, I extract five CCs of blood and inject that into the other user."

"Then what?"

"Once the girls got high, we often turned to sex. You'd understand if you were in the Garden of Eden all day. These girls have sex for a living. They need the smack. The deal is, I offer it for free, and I get a little something on the side."

"Then it's not really free, is it?"

"You know what I mean."

"Yeah, I do. But don't say it's free when it's not."

"Over the last couple of years, as drugs became an addiction at the Garden, sex became mine. Do anything over and over, and eventually, you get desensitized to it. Regular sex just wasn't good enough anymore. I needed something different."

Sarah sipped from her water and waited. He had stopped talking.

"I want to hear everything," she said. "You haven't told me nearly enough."

"Water first. Then I will tell you more."

She rose from her chair, walked over to him, tilted her cup, and splashed the rest of the water into his face. He reared back and gasped.

"What did you do that for?" he yelled.

"Wake the fuck up," she screamed at him. "You're in my house. This is on my terms. I set the rules. You are no longer in control." She got closer to his face. "You're not a cop down here. You're a nobody who's a hair's breadth away from being killed. Talking is all that saves your life, and you're asking for water. How fucking stupid are you?" She slapped his face, then stood back. "Now, keep talking." She walked over to her chair and sat down. "Tell me, weren't you ever afraid of Hepatitis C or HIV when sharing needles?"

He shook his head.

"Oh, right," Sarah said, catching on. "You only got the girls high." She pointed a finger at him. "You never did it yourself, did you?"

He shook his head again.

"And you used protection because, after all, these girls saw lots of men all day long. You lowered your risk of an STD." She rubbed her chin. "What does Deborah think of your business activity?"

"She never liked it but chose to live with it."

"Why would any woman choose to live with that?"

"Money. Our marriage was over years ago. There's a certain amount of hate between us. But she has a nice home and a large monthly budget and is always taken care of."

Sarah wondered how one woman would turn her head as another was abused. Her idealistic view of humanity had decreased over the years. Things like this only made it worse. Barry and Deborah Ashford made her feel a healthy loathing for the human race. They were nothing more than animals who could reason, and even that was defective.

There had to be some good people out there. Even Anne Frank believed that while hiding from the Nazis.

Maybe Sarah needed to get back to Aaron. Spend time with him. He had to be worried about her. She hadn't returned his calls.

"Tell me why you killed Maxine Freeman," Sarah said.

This time he looked up and met her gaze. "I didn't kill Maxine Freeman."

Without a word, Sarah walked over to him and backhanded his face. His head snapped to the side.

"Don't lie to me!" she shouted. "I warned you." She reclaimed her seat. "They found Maxine's body in Bear Creek, five minutes from downtown Kelowna. You dropped her off at the bus depot. Supposedly, Maxine was bound for Halifax. Oh wait, didn't you just warn Lesley the other day that if she didn't come back to work, she could join Maxine in Halifax?"

A trickle of blood seeped out of the corner of his mouth.

"Because Maxine had gone missing, I often used that example to scare my girls back to work. That isn't a crime. I'll admit, it was horrible, but not a crime. And I had nothing to do with Maxine's disappearance or death."

"Then who did? Come on. You expect me to believe that? There are you and drugs and flash-blooding and rape, and you running me off the road. I could've died. You drove away and left me there without checking on me. And by your own admission, you dropped Maxine off at the bus station. No one has seen her in eight months. Funny how her body was found this week. Can't you see your perfect world is unraveling? It's over, but I'm here for you. I'm willing to listen. Confess to me."

"I will say that the flash-blooding and sex was a mistake. I see that now."

"No. It wasn't a mistake. The first time it was a mistake. The second time it was a choice. You can never make the same mistake twice. You chose to continue doing it, knowing full well what you were up to. I can tell by looking at you that you're prurient and not interested in expiation."

"What's prurient and expiation?"

"Prurient is having an excessive interest in sexual matters and activity, and expiation is willing to make amends. You want to be untied and released. You want me arrested and put away. Then you can carry on with your vile ways. Isn't that right? If I go away, would you really shut down the Garden of Eden, apologize to those you've violated, make some kind of amends and then tell the girls to go on their merry way? I highly fucking doubt it. You even offer freebies to your fellow officers. I heard you make a deal with Colin in your driveway the other night. I know all about you."

"How do you know that?" he asked.

"I watch and listen to everything." She pulled out her cell phone and brought up the GPS tracking device. She angled the phone so that he could see it. "That red dot. That's your car. It's still parked at the Garden of Eden. I've been tracking you, following you. Are you so fucking stupid that an amateur could learn all this, but none of your colleagues could? That's why I'm doing what I'm doing because you and your sorry-ass friends at the RCMP don't know how to serve and protect." She got up and paced the floor. "Let's talk about the Geoff Mantler case. The RCMP officer who pulled over Buddy Tavares's car in January 2011. After Mr. Tavares was already on the ground on his hands and knees, doing exactly what the officer told him to do—not resisting arrest— the mountie kicked him in the face, using force that obviously wasn't necessary. Geoff Mantler didn't wait for the RCMP to dismiss him. No, he up and quit the police force." She continued to pace, walking faster now, her energy boosted by anger. "When it finally got to court, the judge gave this ex-cop a fifty-dollar fine, fifty hours of community service, and eighteen months probation. No jail time." She stopped pacing. "Are you fucking kidding me? Geoff Mantler was supposed to police the community to stop violent thugs, and when he became one, the very thing he was supposed to arrest, he got babied in court."

"Are we here because you're upset with a few cops who get caught on camera?"

"We both know much more happens than what's caught on camera. Last week I read a statistic from the National Safety Council that said you're eight times more likely to be killed by a police officer than a terrorist. Can you believe that? And we're all paranoid about terrorism. But you fuckers …" She pointed a finger at him.

The sun was going down. She needed to clear her head and get food. Then she had to park her Jeep up the road. Once the police located it, no one could ever connect it to this house.

"I want you to think about what we've discussed here today. When I get back, I want to hear more. We're going to be at this all night."

"Where are you going?" He sounded worried.

"To buy me some food." She rubbed her stomach. "I'm hungry and thirsty."

"What about me?"

"You get all the food and drink you want when you've told me everything."

She started for the stairs.

"What if something happens to you while you're out? I'll die down here."

"The perils of being an asshole. Dying alone in that chair will be much better than I have planned for you."

At the top of the stairs, she took a deep breath. "How

long can I do this?" she whispered to herself.

Outside, the day's light was fleeing, shoved aside by an ominous darkness.

Under cover of the night, she pulled out of the driveway, maintained the speed limit, and drove to the nearest grocery store. While the police had a vague description of her, the exposure was minimal but necessary.

After this, she wouldn't need to leave the house for days, and since Barry was her target all along, she was done in Kelowna. But what was Vivian referring to when she said Barry was the barnacle on the mother ship?

What mother lode of information was Barry holding back?

Something told Sarah she would find out soon enough.

Or she would torture the bastard until she killed him because she was absolutely done with anyone thinking they could get away with rape.

Chapter 22

Deborah watched as Sarah pulled out of the driveway next door. She waited until the Jeep's taillights disappeared down the road before she headed to Barry's gun cabinet.

Once she got inside the cabinet, she selected his favorite weapon. She would never forget how he pulled over a car at three in the morning. The two teens were headed to a party, but they'd had too much to drink, and it was Barry and his partner's job to bring them downtown to the drunk tank.

Once the driver and his passengers were in the cruiser, something caught Barry's attention between the front seats of the teens' car. After fumbling for a moment, his hand stuck against the center console, he pulled up a Colt revolver. He later learned it was a Walker Colt Replica. It had been modified to shoot the bullets in it, but she couldn't remember the name of what kind of bullets were in what gun. All she could recall was the name of this gun because Barry had stolen it that day and talked about it to her hundreds of times. He always kept it loaded in the locked cabinet.

She entered her bedroom, opened the closet, and retrieved Joan's front door keys from the small lockbox where she kept all the neighbors' keys.

She still didn't know what Sarah was up to, but Sarah had kidnapped her husband. The fact that Deborah had keys to Joan's house was probably lost on Sarah, even though she was told that Deborah was the one who came to check on the previous tenants, Jacob and his girlfriend, as Joan had asked her to.

How much time did she have? Sarah had been gone for at least three minutes now. Deborah guessed she had a minimum of twenty minutes.

She used her back door, scooted around to the front of the house, the Colt hidden behind her leg, and made her way, as casually as she could, to the front door of Joan's house. The Rankins next door were gone. The only other house was half a block down on the other side of Deborah's house, leaving no one close enough to see what she was doing. She rationalized that she could only get caught if Sarah came home while she was still inside.

She turned the key and opened the front door to Joan and Mike's house.

"Hello?" she called. "Anyone home?"

She crossed the threshold. It was dark. All the lights were out. A chill coursed through her. Goosebumps rose on her arms, and she shuddered.

With her free hand, she turned on the hallway light.

Nothing in the living room looked any different from the last time she had been there.

"Hello?" she called louder. "Barry? You in here?"

"Debbie?" His voice came from somewhere in the house. Maybe the basement.

"Debbie!" he shouted louder.

"Where are you?" she shouted back.

"Basement."

Deborah left the front door ajar as she started for the basement. Barry hated basements. He refused to enter theirs unless absolutely necessary. It had something to do with his childhood, but she had never heard the entire story.

Her curiosity made her smile. What could Sarah have been thinking? Barry was an RCMP officer. She would be in a lot of trouble when this came out. But the side of Deborah that hated her husband and the monster he had become held out hope that Sarah somehow hurt him. He had to be secured in some way too. Otherwise, he would've walked upstairs and left under his own power.

"Are you alone?" she called down the stairs.

"Yes," he said, a tone of weakness in his voice she hadn't heard before.

She took the stairs one at a time, knowing she still had time. And she had a gun. As observant as she had been, Sarah hadn't appeared armed.

Deborah stopped at the bottom of the stairs and stared at her husband. He was strapped to a metal chair with duct tape. He had a ball of white and red paper towels wrapped around one hand and was as pale as a white sheet. With his hair dampened by sweat, he didn't just look deathly pale, he looked near death.

"What happened here?" Debbie asked.

"How did you know to come over?"

"I saw Sarah bring you inside this house. You were only wearing underwear, and your hands were bound. I had no idea …" she trailed off. "I waited because I wasn't sure … is this supposed to be some kind of sex game? Does Sarah work in the Garden of Eden? Because if I'm intruding, I'll just leave now. I don't want to watch this kind of debauchery."

He rolled his head back and forth. "Sarah is a vile woman. She kidnapped me, brought me here, and tortured me." He nodded at the floor beside him. "That's my finger." His eyes watered when he looked up at her. "Sarah hacked it off."

She gasped and coughed to cover up a smile. "What?" She tried to sound shocked and mortified, but it wasn't working. It came out in a giggle like she laughed the word.

Whatever you did, it serves you right.

"Something funny?" Barry asked. "Untie me. Cut this fucking tape. Get me out of here before that crazy lunatic bitch comes back."

"Where has she gone?" Debbie asked as she moved farther into the room.

"To buy groceries. Can you believe it? Torture me, cut off my finger, slap me around, and then get some food. This girl is psycho. Look, honey." He glanced up at her, his eyes pleading. "Cut me loose. I'm really thirsty. We need to go and call the police. Ever since this girl showed up at the beach the other day, she has harassed me. Now she's torturing me. She said that I would beg her to paralyze me when she was done with me to stop the pain. 'Paralysis would be mercy,' she said, or something like that."

"Why is she doing this?" Debbie asked as she moved to stand in front of her husband. "What did you do to her? Or is this just for fun?"

"She's asking me all these insane questions about my life and the parlor." He swallowed hard. "Look, I'm really thirsty."

"In a second. What kind of questions?"

"What does it matter?" He met her eyes and studied them for a moment. "You're starting to sound like her. And what's with my Colt? Why do you have it?"

"Protection. If a girl will kidnap a cop, there's no telling what she's capable of. What else have you two talked about?"

"She thinks I killed Maxine Freeman. Crazy, eh?"

"Yeah, totally crazy."

She raised the Colt and leveled it, the barrel aimed at her husband's forehead.

"Hey, what are you doing—"

He didn't get to finish his sentence. The bullet tore through his left eye, opening a hole that widened enough to expose bone above his nose. Brain matter and blood shot from the back of his head. For a brief second, his head stayed up—suspended in a slow-motion pantomime of a bobblehead on strained neck muscles—before it dropped, and his jaw bounced once off his chest before coming still.

To be sure he was dead, Debbie fired two more times. Once in the chest, roughly in the location of his heart, and another in his groin. The distance between them was such that she didn't need to worry about aiming properly to hit him where she wanted. The bullet in the groin was not so much to make sure he was dead as to throw off the police.

Now they would be looking for a vengeful killer. One who hated Barry so much that even after he was dead, they had to shoot him in the cock.

Barry must have raped the shooter at one time or another.

There's no way his loving wife would ever kill her own husband.

Especially not in such a vile, angry way. And not in Joan and Mike's house, where Sarah was the tenant. The same Sarah who had been seen taking the half-naked and bound RCMP officer from her vehicle into this house.

"It's perfect," she said to herself. "I get rid of my husband, and Sarah takes the fall."

She wrapped her hand in a paper towel and picked up the handsaw. Then she went to work on her husband's legs. An experienced cutter, she sliced along the top of his thighs where they attached to the base of his hips. At the bone, the handsaw wasn't enough. Within two minutes, she found an ax in the storeroom and hacked Barry's legs off with ease. She dropped the ax on the floor, wrapped the exposed ends with paper towels, and secured the paper towels with the duct tape Sarah had supplied. Then she took her husband's legs and ran from the room, one under each arm.

Deborah left the house the way she came in but didn't turn off the lights or lock the front door.

The police would need access to the house as soon as they arrived.

After placing Barry's legs in the bathtub in her basement bathroom, she stepped back outside and walked down the embankment toward the beach. At the water, she wiped her fingerprints off the Colt and tossed it as far as she could into the lake.

When she got upstairs, and into her house, Sarah still wasn't home.

She poured a glass of wine, turned on some soft jazz

music, and picked up the phone.

A woman answered and asked, "Do you require police, fire, or ambulance?"

"Police."

The line clicked.

"Police. What's the emergency?"

"My neighbor."

"What's your neighbor doing, ma'am?"

"Something awful, I'm sure. My name is Deborah Ashford. I'm Barry's wife up here on Bennett Road."

"Oh, hi Debbie, it's Bob. What's happening?"

"Bob, you know that picture of the girl that was circulated in the news earlier?"

"Yeah, the girl we're looking for."

"I think she lives next door."

"Really?"

"I saw her come home earlier, and she had someone with her."

"You want a unit to respond?"

"Maybe after what I tell you next. She took someone inside her house. This man was only wearing underwear, and his hands were bound. He had a shirt tied around his head."

"Oh, that sounds like …"

"I just heard a couple of gunshots next door, and I haven't been able to raise my husband on his phone. Could you send everything available? I'm kinda scared over here. I'm all alone."

"Hold on, Mrs. Ashford." Bob's voice turned cold, less friendly. "We're on our way."

Deborah smiled.

She sipped her wine.

Chapter 23

When the door opened again, Detective Lang didn't have a phone book with him. Another man entered the small room with Lang. He wore a similar suit and identified himself, but Greg immediately forgot his name.

"Greg, you don't have to say anything until your lawyer gets here. But we want to share something with you. Fair enough?"

Greg didn't respond. Lang took that as an answer.

"Okay. Here's what we have." Lang sat down across from him and clasped his hands together. "We have you arguing at the front door of the Garden of Eden. You assaulted Nate Ferrey—"

"That's his name?" Greg asked, smiling. "Ferrey?"

"Why is that funny?" Lang asked.

"You know, for such a big guy. Working as a bouncer. And his name is Ferrey." They weren't amused. "Forget about it. You were saying?"

"After you left the premises, Nate claims to have called his boss, Barry Ashford. When Barry arrived, he pulled his employee into the back room to talk about why her brother was causing so much trouble."

Greg felt the loss and loneliness like it was something he could touch. If Lesley had died, he probably would've killed Barry Ashford.

"That man wasn't just talking to her. As everyone in this room already knows."

"Your sister is now recovering at the hospital. We can't say for certain what happened in that back room. How do we know she didn't do that to herself before Barry got there?"

Greg wanted to add that Barry was dressed in underwear when he and Sarah barged in, but Lang raised a hand, staying his protest.

"Just let me finish." He adjusted his jacket and placed his hands on the table. "When you returned to the massage studio, you had a girl with you."

Yeah, my hero.

"What is her name?" Lang asked.

Greg remained silent.

"Okay, can you tell me what the plan was?"

Greg looked down at his hands. He brushed a piece of lint off his pants.

"In the time that you took your sister to the hospital, the girl you entered Barry's place of business with tied Barry's hands together. She wrapped a shirt around his head and walked him outside, pushing him into the back of a Jeep Cherokee. We have two witnesses who saw your friend kidnap an RCMP officer. Barry hasn't been seen since and hasn't been answering his phone. His car is still parked outside the Garden of Eden. We have every available officer looking for the girl in the Jeep. Do you know how serious this is? Do you know what aiding and abetting means?"

As Lang talked, Greg's stomach sickened. What could Sarah have done? It was one thing to beat the guy for what he did to Lesley, but kidnap him? An RCMP officer? What was her plan?

"Are you at least willing to tell us her name?"

Greg stayed quiet, too scared to talk now.

"You're aware that you will be charged with whatever she gets charged with when we figure this all out? You two walked in together. You pulled Lesley out. Then, instead of calling us, that girl abducted a cop." Detective Lang slammed his hands down on the table, making Greg jump in his seat. "Tell me where she is. Tell me where she has taken Barry Ashford."

Greg was cowed into silence. He would never speak without a lawyer present.

"We also have her BMW motorcycle. She ditched it off Sexsmith Road. It has California license plates. We should have her name as soon as we hear back from the DMV down there."

Someone knocked. The door opened. A woman stuck her head in.

"What?" Lang asked.

"A call."

"Tell them I'm busy."

"You're going to want to take this."

"Why?" Lang asked, not taking his eyes off Greg.

"It's Barry's wife, Deborah. She just saw a girl in a Jeep

Cherokee take a man into the house next door to hers. His hands were tied, and he wore a shirt over his face."

Lang turned to the woman at the door. "Are you serious?"

The woman nodded rapidly.

Detective Lang got out of his chair and almost jumped at the door.

"Lock this door. He does not leave. Clear?"

"Clear."

The door shut after both men had exited. Greg was alone.

"What the hell have you done, Sarah?" he whispered. "What have *I* done?"

Chapter 24

SARAH HAD PICKED UP what she needed and was on her way back when a tickling sensation crossed the back of her neck. An inauspicious premonition. As if a spider caused her to shiver as it crawled along her flesh. But the premonition wasn't strong enough for her to cut and run. She couldn't walk away and leave Barry tied up in her basement. Too many unanswered questions. She had to find out why she was here and what Vivian wanted from her. Vivian wouldn't have brought her this far just to make her lose it all and end up in jail. There was a darker truth that needed to be revealed.

Even though she didn't see any cops, she kept her speed down.

She reminded herself that no one knew where she was. Under pressure, Greg Wright could be a risk, but even he didn't know where she lived.

Five minutes later, as she drove along McKinley Road, minutes from home, she realized they could find her house through Greg. She had hired his company to do housecleaning. Derek, Greg's employee, had come out to walk around the house and produce an estimate. Sarah's address was on Greg's books, and Greg was aware of this from when they had talked at the pub the day he had followed her.

But would Greg tell the cops where she lived after Sarah had helped get his sister out of the Garden of Eden? There was no easy answer. But one thing was for sure; she couldn't rely on anyone. If Greg was a weak link, she had to consider the possibility that the police were on their way or waiting for her.

The bag of food and carton of distilled water on the seat beside her would last at least three days. Maybe the Rankins next door wouldn't mind her visiting their house while they were away.

She parked on a side road, grabbed the bag and the water, and headed toward her house. Greg's gun was safely in her waistband. At any sign of the police, she would have to leave. She could make it on her own for a couple of days until the local authorities worked out all the details. Then she would turn herself in and tell her side. Her reputation would go a long way to help clear her name.

But she hoped it wouldn't come to that. Vivian had an end game, and it was Sarah's job to trust the process until she figured out where Vivian was leading her.

As she approached the end of Bennett Road, she saw the Rankins' house silhouetted in the dark. To her right, Barry's house had a couple of lights on inside. As far as she could tell, Deborah wasn't peeking out any of the windows.

As she passed Barry's driveway, the front of her house came into view.

She almost dropped the bag of food.

The inside light was on, and the front door was open.

She stopped and listened. Nothing moved in the dark.

Did he untie himself? If it wasn't Barry, then why weren't the police here? Unless the intruder is still inside.

Sarah ran for the Rankins's house. She tried the locked garage window, but it wouldn't budge. Then she moved around to the back. The sliding glass door that led out onto the deck was unlocked. She remembered something from a conversation about Joan's previous tenant breaking into the Rankins' house. Debbie was supposed to get their door fixed since the Rankins were still out of town.

She slid the door aside and stepped in. A dank odor assaulted her nose. She dropped her bag of food and her bottle of water and pulled out Greg's gun. After sliding the glass door shut, she headed for the front door of her rental home.

No police sirens pierced the night. Only crickets and the sounds of summer joined her as she walked to her front door. With every nerve-tingling, she checked behind her before entering the house. She pushed her front door open the rest of the way and stepped inside. Her computer was where she'd left it. Nothing seemed to be touched.

She waited and listened to the house. With her back to the front closet, she closed her eyes and focused on her ears.

Nothing. Not even a faucet dripped.

She made her way through the kitchen, softly planting every step on the Italian tile floor.

She took one more check over her shoulder at the living room and kitchen and then started down the stairs, Greg's gun leading the way.

When she got to the bottom of the stairs, she gasped. Her knees almost gave out. A sudden rush of what she was looking at and the consequences flooded her consciousness.

Barry Ashford was dead.

But not just dead. Mutilated. The upper part of his body was still affixed to the metal chair.

She moved closer and walked around the body. Someone had shot Barry several times and cut his legs off at the base of his underwear.

Who could do such a thing?

The implications of this were too horrible to comprehend. There were people who saw her take him in her Jeep. Her fingerprints were all over the place. She had rented this house and prepared the basement for Barry's interrogation.

But never to actually kill him.

That was all threatened in the effort to gain the truth from him. The darker truth.

Unless Barry's killer was that darker truth Vivian spoke of.

Whoever it was had used this opportunity to break into her house, kill Barry and make it look like Sarah had done it.

Her cell phone vibrated.

She took a quick peek.

Aaron.

She slipped the phone away. Not now. Maybe in a few days when this was all over, but not now.

Who could have done this to Barry, and who knew he

was here?

Greg and Lesley Wright.

They were the only ones she could think of.

But wouldn't they involve the police now that Barry was dead?

As if to answer her question, the distant sound of a police siren filtered down to her from outside.

She had to leave. There was no time to review the DVR. No time to discover who had done this. Cops don't respond well to the murder of one of their own. Especially not one murdered in such a brutal fashion. If she were found inside by the body, it would probably result in her own murder.

She ran for the stairs, knowing that whoever did this could still be in the house. She stopped at the top of the stairs and glanced around the corner. Her kitchen and living room were still empty, but now red and blue lights flashed across the walls.

They were outside, but they hadn't shouted for her to come out yet.

She grabbed her laptop and cord, slipped the gun into the back of her pants, and ran onto the back deck.

"Sarah," someone yelled from the front of the house.

She jumped over the deck's railing and landed hard. She almost twisted an ankle but caught herself and ran for the Rankins's house.

As she entered the sliding door at the Rankins' house, she heard them shout her name again.

She set her computer down and found a broom in the laundry room. She twisted the end off, discarded it, and used the pole to secure the defective sliding door so no one else could follow her inside.

In the dark, she used her hands as eyes as she walked through the Rankins' unfamiliar house, navigating her way upstairs until she could look through their blinds at the action taking place outside.

Under the large bay window at the front of the Rankins' house, two small ones were used to help ventilate the room on hot summer days. She opened the one on the right, sat on their carpeted living room floor, shoulder against the wall, ear to the screen, and listened to the frenzy of activity as they discovered Barry Ashford's mutilated corpse in her basement.

Deborah Ashford exited her own house. When three RCMP officers surrounded her, she nearly fell over, but one of the men caught her. It would be horrible to learn of her husband's death this way.

More sirens approached.

A man dressed in a suit and tie walked toward the Rankins' driveway. He spoke rapidly into a cell phone. Something about charging Greg Wright as an accomplice to first-degree murder.

Sarah's stomach dropped.

Accomplice? Wasn't he involved in Barry's murder? If Greg didn't do it, then who killed Barry?

"Yeah, I understand," the man shouted into the phone. "Greg has been in custody ever since he was picked up at the hospital. Barry's body was just found in Sarah's basement." The man choked back a sob and wiped at his face. "He's torn apart, man. His fucking legs were cut off. I mean, who does that sort of thing? Greg helped Sarah abduct Barry. He goes down for this, too."

The man turned toward the arriving ambulance.

The noise of the sirens blocked most of what he was

saying, but Sarah caught a few words like, *kill her*, and *she will die for this.*

She didn't have to hear it all to know what any cop would think and say when one of their own was cut down in such a horrific way.

"Hey, sis," Sarah whispered. "You think you could help me out here? I might be in a lot of trouble. The way things are looking, I don't see a way out."

When no numbing came, no sign of a message, Sarah understood she was on her own. She had to believe that Vivian had not abandoned her, only that Sarah was on the right path.

As crazy as that sounded, she had to stay on the right path.

At least, that was what she wanted to believe.

The alternative meant death by cop or a Canadian prison for a long time.

Chapter 25

THE DOOR TO THE small room banged open so hard it bounced off the wall, and Detective Lang had to grab it before it smacked back into him.

"Guess what?" Lang shouted.

Greg raised both hands. "What?"

"Your friend, Sarah, is now being hunted for first-degree murder."

That hit Greg as hard as a fist to the solar plexus. This time when he spoke, it wasn't as cocky. "What?"

The detective slammed the door shut behind him and walked up to the table, bumping it with his thigh.

"RCMP Officer Barry Ashford has been found dead and mutilated in the basement of a house Sarah was renting. He was shot three times, and then someone cut his finger off and both his legs." He leaned closer to Greg, his hands flat on the table. "Did you hear me? Cut his fucking legs off. They're missing. She stole his legs. Can you believe it?" He leaned back.

"I, ahh, what?" Greg couldn't find his voice. What did that mean for him? How could Sarah have done that? And why the hell would she cut his legs off?

"And you know what the creepy thing is?" Lang asked.

Greg offered a blank stare as a response.

"It was Barry's wife that saw Sarah enter her house with Barry's wrists tied and a shirt over his head. She called it in. When we got there, Barry was already dead."

"Why are you telling me—"

"Because the charges against you just increased to you being an accomplice to murder," Lang shouted. "You entered The Garden of Eden together. Barry was kidnapped and murdered. You're as guilty as she is." The detective rolled his tongue around in his mouth and spit a gob of phlegm on the floor. "A cop was killed tonight, and it's your fault as much as the woman who killed him. You're finished. Done for. You will never live a normal life again. You had better stop stalling and start talking, or you might die in here." Lang turned to the two-way glass. "Turn that thing back on."

When he returned his gaze to Greg, the rage on his reddened face was as if Lucifer smiled back at him. His blood cooled, and he wondered if he would die in the interrogation room chair.

"I'll talk." Greg found his voice.

The detective pulled out a chair and sat. "Start talking and telling. Tell me everything. Start at the beginning."

"It all started in the Garden of Eden—"

"Seriously? You want to joke with me?"

Greg cleared his throat. "No, I'm serious, the Garden of

Eden Massage Studio. I wasn't talking about creation theory."

Lang tilted his head. "Of course. I knew what you meant. Carry on."

"Can I have a water?"

"Water!" the detective yelled.

The door opened a moment later, and the girl who had interrupted them before about the phone call stepped in, set a glass on the table, and promptly left without setting eyes on Greg.

He drank half the glass in three gulps, placed it on the table, and told the detective everything, going over all the details of Lesley's violation, the flash-blooding events in the back of the Garden of Eden, all the way up to Maxine Freeman's disappearance and the recent discovery of her body. He concluded with why Lesley tried to kill herself on the bridge a few days ago and how Barry was helping her along with her suicide when they broke into the back room of the Garden of Eden.

"I did nothing wrong," Greg said. "All I've ever tried to do was keep my business afloat, stay out of trouble, and steer my sister from the Garden of Eden. But Barry kept pulling her back in. The break-ins were all him. He stole my company records and only broke into homes my company cleans." Greg looked down at his hands. "It was all his fault. But I never meant for anyone to be killed." He looked up. "That's not in me. If it were, I would've shot Barry when I saw him about to rape my sister."

Detective Lang got up from the table and walked to the door.

"That's all I need. Thank you, Greg. You've been a big

help."

"So, can I leave?"

"All you've done is tell us why you wanted Barry killed. It's a little thing we call motive. You also told us how you did it by recruiting a female hitman from the States." The detective clapped his hands. "Well done." He almost shut the door, then stopped. "To answer your question. You can leave this building when you're shackled and suited up for the maximum security facility where you'll meet your new girlfriend, Bruce." He shook his head. "Fucking pathetic." He closed the door, and the lock clicked.

Then Greg cried.

Chapter 26

Sarah monitored the activity in the front of her house throughout the initial hours from the Rankins' living room floor, until eventually, somewhere after midnight, when the emergency vehicles, the coroner, and friends and family of Deborah Ashford departed the area, leaving one unmarked cruiser parked down the road.

Despondent and unaware of Vivian's intentions, Sarah moved through the Rankins' house without turning on any lights until she got downstairs to her computer. She took it inside the windowless laundry room, off the main basement, and plugged it in. Just in case a small amount of glare from her screen fed through the base of the door, she laid a towel down.

Once she found an unlocked internet signal, she logged on and began browsing local news websites. Castanet was featuring a live update to the tragedy. The loss of a hero, the article said. The man who pulled a suicide victim from the lake only a few days ago has been found murdered in McKinley Landing. Reports indicated that the decorated police officer had been mutilated. The police were looking for Sarah Roberts, an American woman in her mid-twenties.

They had a picture of her downed BMW bike.

All her loved ones would now know that she was wanted for murder. Aaron and Parkman might show up. Her parents might come, which was exactly what she didn't want. No more rescuing. She needed to work with her sister without outside help. Vivian had to deliver the information to Sarah in a way that didn't involve others because it was too dangerous. Aaron and Parkman couldn't continue to come running every time something went wrong. It made her feel like a lost teenager or a stray dog.

Her phone vibrated.

Aaron.

She had to answer this time. If she didn't, he would come for sure.

"Hi," she said. "What time is it there?"

"Hey. It's almost four in the morning."

Hearing his voice sent a warmth through her, a longing that made her want him, want his strong arms wrapped around her. Maybe this had been a mistake. Maybe being away from him wasn't healing her. It was hurting her.

"You okay?" he asked.

"Yeah."

"Bad time?"

"No."

"I've called a few times," he said.

"I know."

Silence. He probably expected more from her, but she wasn't in a giving mood. Images of Barry's corpse, sans legs, flitted through her mind.

"You need me in Kelowna?" he asked.

If you only knew.

"I'm okay," she said.

"Sarah?"

"Yeah?"

"I'm reading the news."

"Good for you. Helps one keep up with world affairs."

"Sarah?"

"Yeah?"

"This is Aaron."

"I know."

"Keep the smartass stuff for assholes who aren't smart."

"Okay."

"You're in the news."

"Probably. When am I not?"

"Sarah."

She waited. Almost a minute went by.

Then he said, in a soft, velvety whisper, "I love you."

And she broke down.

He waited until her tears were whimpers and not wracking sobs as they were for a few minutes.

"Can I come and help?" he asked.

"No."

"Why not?"

"Because this is something Vivian and I have to do."

"How are you going to solve murder charges?"

"Is that what the news is saying?"

"You're somewhat of a big name in Toronto. When the

Toronto papers got wind of what was happening in Kelowna, they ran with it. A dead cop? In the house you rented? Witnesses claim to have seen you kidnap this guy from his business. The guy's wife saw you force him into the house. Now you're missing, and every cop in the country is looking for you. I'd say it looked planned and executed diligently, which means you need help."

"I didn't do it."

"I know that, but they don't. And unless you arrange to turn yourself in, with a lawyer present, cops are liable to shoot on sight."

"Someone else walked in the house and did it while I was buying groceries."

"They won't like that."

"What?"

"Groceries aren't a good defense. They won't like that someone walked into your rented house and shot and mutilated this guy while you were out getting something to eat. You'll need more."

"I know."

"What's Vivian say about this?"

"Nothing yet."

"Seems to me she got you into this; she'll get you out. There've been times when things have looked terrible, but it all worked out. It always does."

"That's what I'm hoping for."

"Where are you now?"

"Hiding."

"You're not going to tell me?"

"Does it matter? You're not here. You're not coming over for coffee. Telling you makes no difference. Unless you're coming to help, which I don't want."

During the silence that followed, an idea came to her.

"Aaron, who said the axiom, 'Knowledge is power'?"

"I think that was Francis Bacon."

"Isn't knowledge just having information? It's intelligence when you can use that knowledge. It's wisdom when you keep true to yourself while using it."

"Sounds good. What's your point?"

"I think I just figured out who killed the cop. I already had the information, but I wasn't using it right, and I wasn't me. I was lost for a bit. I'm not used to antagonizing people without knowing why. Standing up for what's right and fighting for the underdog, that's me. But outright going after someone without provocation was hard."

"You're losing me. And scaring me. What's that about being lost?"

"Nothing. I have to go."

"Wait. What are you going to do?"

"Clear this up."

"How?"

"Watch the news."

"That's not fair."

"I'm sorry, Aaron. But I need to handle this." For a moment, she only caught his breathing on the phone. "I miss you."

"I miss you, too."

"Aaron?"

"Yeah?"

"I'll come home when this is over." She paused for a second. "If you still want me after what I did to Parkman."

"Want you? I would die for you, as would Parkman.

When are you going to get it? Are you fucked?"

"Then I'll come home."

"That's what I called to hear. Those are nice words. And Sarah?"

"Yeah?"

"Make sure you come home in one piece."

"I'll do my best. Gotta go."

She clicked off before she broke down again. She powered down her computer and moved into the basement, where she lay on the sofa in the dark.

She fell asleep sometime after three in the morning, her eyes wet with tears, her mind on Aaron when it wasn't on the one person who had keys to the Rankins's house when they were away. The same person who had keys to the house Sarah rented. The same person who checked on the previous tenants for Sarah's landlords when they mysteriously disappeared.

Deborah Ashford.

She was the only person with access. There had been no sign of forced entry at Sarah's house. No one broke in. Someone had used a key, walked downstairs, shot Barry, and cut him up. A certain someone who probably hated all the women he had sex with regularly. The woman who benefitted financially from his death.

And she had the perfect scapegoat: Sarah Roberts, the stranger from the States who had been seen around town antagonizing Barry and who had recently kidnapped him.

Funny how it was the nosy neighbor who saw Sarah take Barry into the house.

Deborah had waited until Sarah left the house to make her move.

So Sarah would wait until everyone was gone before she made her move.

And this time, she wouldn't play nice.

The DVR in the basement would reveal who killed Barry, but Sarah would also get a confession from Deborah Ashford.

She fell asleep with newfound hope.

Within days, she would be vindicated, and she didn't need Aaron or Parkman to come to her aid.

She had also discovered the mother lode.

Deborah Ashford, a cop's wife, was a murderer.

Barry was the barnacle, and Deborah was the mother ship.

Chapter 27

Something tugged on Sarah's feet. The stress and exhaustion of the past few days had caused her to have dreams of violence. Twice she woke in the darkness, unaware of her surroundings. But no flashlights pointed in her face, and nothing moved outside the curtains by the sliding door, so she fell back to sleep.

The tugging on her feet became persistent. There was a burning at the base of her neck, too. She woke up fully and opened her eyes. The sun bore down on her. She had to close her eyes again and cover her face with her arms.

The realization that someone had pulled the curtains back made her snap her eyes open and looked around.

A thick rope had been wrapped around each ankle. Something choked her when she pulled on them and tried to get up. Her hands were still free. She used them to examine the rope around her neck. It had no play, and as long as she remained lying still, with her head on the armrest of the couch, the rope didn't choke her.

Who had done this? How did I sleep through it?

Deborah Ashford stepped into view and looked down at her. "Ah, she wakes."

"What have you done to me?" Sarah asked.

"Actually, I'm surprised the drugs wore off as fast as they did."

"Drugs?"

Deborah pulled a capped syringe from her pants pocket. "A little something to keep you sleeping while I tied up loose ends."

Sarah struggled for a moment, then lay back on the couch, stared at the ceiling, and breathed deeply.

"I do wonder, though." Deborah walked to a small window at the side of the room and pulled the curtains back. Since the Rankins' house was the last one on the street and their lot pied out, this side window had a view of Sarah's and Deborah's house. "Why the fixation with my husband?"

"What are we doing here?" Sarah asked. "The police think I killed your husband. You've drugged me and tied me up. When should we expect them to come running through the front door?"

Deborah let the curtain fall back into place, but she didn't turn around right away. "Oh, I don't think we need the police." When she turned around, her eyes held a gleam of madness. "Do you?"

Deborah Ashford, a murderer who mutilated her husband in the house next door, walked over to Sarah and looked down at her, a definite insanity in her eyes.

"You figured it out, didn't you?" Deborah asked.

"Figured what out?" Sarah tested the limits of the ropes again. Her feet were locked down, slightly spread apart. Deborah must have secured each ankle to the front and back leg of the couch. Unless Sarah had the strength to pull straight up hard enough to break the leg of the couch, her feet weren't going anywhere.

The same for her neck. The ends were probably tied to the legs and then looped around her neck. There wasn't even enough play to lower her chin under it and slide the rope over her head. Her free hands could literally do nothing.

"*Figure out what?*" Deborah mocked Sarah in a child's voice. "You figured out what happened to Jacob and his girlfriend, the previous tenants in Joan and Mike's house, that's what."

Suddenly, as if knowledge was a surfboard, the wave came in, and Sarah rode it to shore. Everything came together. Every piece, every detail.

Jacob and his girlfriend were missing. The Rankins were not home, although normally they were at this time of year. Maxine Freeman was recently found with body parts missing. Deborah Ashford had been murdering people for quite some time and getting away with it. But where had she been storing the bodies?

"I see you understand who I am and what I am capable of," Deborah said. "But you only have half the story."

"Which half?"

"The nicer half."

"Somehow, I don't think so."

Deborah moved closer, taking each step slowly like she walked to a wedding march. When she hovered over Sarah, she leaned down close enough for Sarah to smell her rank breath.

"You may think there are things I'm incapable of." Deborah's mouth made wet sounds as she formed her words. She licked her lips, moistening them. "You would be wrong." She stood and returned to the window, where she sat in a chair.

The Rankins had turned their walk-out basement into a theater room with two chairs and the couch Sarah was on, placed in the main viewing area. Track lighting hung from the ceiling tiles, and a gas fireplace was surrounded by rock under what looked like a fifty-inch TV.

But what happened to the Rankins?

Last night's call to Aaron ended without her allowing him to help. He would have no idea where she was and the trouble she was in. Parkman was in Santa Rosa, busy with his private investigation practice.

She was completely on her own unless Vivian thought of some way to help. Although that would be tricky because Sarah wasn't in a position to write anything down.

To stall for time, she asked, "How did you do it?"

"Do what?" Deborah whispered without turning around.

"All the killings."

"I should be asking you a thing or two." Deborah crossed her legs and faced Sarah, letting the curtain she was peeking through fall back into place.

"What are you watching out there?" Sarah asked.

"I told the police that I want to grieve in peace. I'm waiting for the last cruiser to leave." She smiled wide. "Then we will truly be alone."

"What if I scream?"

"Go ahead. They won't hear you. I'm waiting until they

leave to retrieve my husband's legs and bring them here. The Rankins have two large freezers." The crazy stare, one eye twitching, gave Sarah goosebumps. "Once you and I get started, I don't want to have to watch what they're up to. It'll just be you and me at the end of this dead-end street, at least a dozen houses from the next person. We will be quite alone, and you'll be able to scream all you want."

Sarah's stomach twitched. She had been through a lot in her young life, but when faced with someone so evil and calculating, someone with such lavish plans and gruesome ideas, and no obvious way for Sarah to escape, her body responded on a chemical level. Her stomach filled with adrenaline, her legs began to shake, and her mouth dried up. She needed hope. Hope to get out of this in one piece. Hope to make things right with the authorities. Hope to stay alive and see Aaron again. Just hope.

Normally it was her attitude that wore her opponent down or her ability to fight and outthink her opponent, but Deborah didn't look or act like the kind of person Sarah could wear down easily.

"You're insane. I should have seen it the night we met."

"Yes," Deborah giggled. "Quite."

"Why kill the previous tenants?"

"They broke into this house."

"They did?"

"Jacob followed me one day. I think he saw me come in with my key. The key the Rankins gave me, I might add. But Jacob had become suspicious of the Rankins's whereabouts. He couldn't get in the house, so he came around back here and broke in through the same door you used. When he saw what I had done to the Rankins, let's just say he got sick.

Threw up over there." She pointed to the side wall by the door, then threw her hands in the air in a dramatic flair. "My secret was out. That left me with no choice." Her face changed to a dead stare.

"So you kill people who discover who you are?"

She nodded and checked a fingernail, now acting as if their discussion bored her.

"Who exactly are you?" Sarah asked, already tired of the histrionics.

"Your worst nightmare."

Sarah giggled. "So you're a cliché?" She clucked her tongue. "You're nothing more than a kidnapper and a murderer. I've met worse."

Deborah stopped with the fingernail. She leaned forward and glared at Sarah.

"No. You. Haven't. Met. Worse." Her lips didn't move. The sounds emanated from her mouth like they were cast in marble, as hard as her soul. Her composure changed to relative calm, and her voice returned to normal when she said, "Ever heard of Rick Gibson?"

"Can't say that I have."

Sarah pulled and then pushed forward with each ankle, but neither one would budge. She couldn't grab the rope around her neck and lift it over her head. With her knees bent the way they were, even if she somehow got to her feet, she would be too bent over and too far off balance to be able to hop away.

"I'll never forget the day Rick Gibson stood on the steps of the Vancouver Court House and ate that human testicle."

"What?" Sarah stopped moving. She wasn't sure she heard her right. "Did you say human testicle?"

Deborah looked up at nothing on the ceiling. "It was September 22, 1989. I remember it well. In July of that year, the Vancouver police had confiscated the testicle when Mr. Gibson tried to eat it at the Pitt International Gallery." Deborah brought her attention down to Sarah. She looked at her with those glaring eyes. "You see, Rick was an artist and was allowed to publicly eat a human testicle in London just a few months before that. Back in 1988, he ate human tonsils in London. But no, come to Canada, and suddenly you can't eat whatever you want." She wagged a finger. "But the police in Vancouver had to give him back his testicle, and he ate it on their court steps. I was there to cheer him on. I watched him eat it. I admired him. I wanted to be like him." She waved her arms around, almost pinwheeling. "There's no crime in that, now is there?"

Sarah looked away, disgusted.

Is cannibalism the mother lode, Vivian? A little advance notice would've helped. Kinda stuck here now. Warm meat is held hostage by a cannibal. You gotta fix this, Vivian, or I'm going to get eaten for breakfast.

"How about Lamia?" Deborah asked. She checked outside through the curtain, then let it fall back. "Ever read any Greek Mythology?"

Sarah's quick responses and usual wit dried up in the face of possibly becoming Deborah's next meal.

Deborah was talking again. "Lamia was Zeus' mistress. She was the beautiful queen of Libya who became a child-eating demon. Her name even came from the Greek word for gullet, *laimos.* Hera, Zeus' wife, grew jealous and killed all of Lamia's children, turning Lamia into a monster that devoured the children of others. Sad story."

"True," Sarah admitted. "Sad story, but it's a myth."

"John Keats composed a poem about her in 1819. He described Lamia as having the tale of a serpent. I'm sure Lamia's story even inspired Hansel and Gretel. What about vampires? Isn't that a cannibal story? Consuming one's blood?"

"Myths," Sarah said. "Fables. Stories that are made up to scare people."

"Did you know that the average human adult has almost 80,000 dietary calories? There once was a website called the Cannibal Café that has since been taken down. I can tell you from experience that the thigh muscle is as good as any veal. Maybe a little older than veal, but definitely not a steak."

Sarah swiveled her head, the rope softly rubbing her skin. She hoped she wouldn't throw up and then choke on it. "Why tell me all this?"

"I like my food to know what will become of it."

That's it. I'm going to throw up. Then I'm going to kill Deborah with my mouth. See how she likes to be torn apart with teeth. All I need is for her to get close enough.

"We all do it," Deborah added.

Sarah breathed a short laugh out through her nose. "How so?"

"Self-cannibalism is done by swallowing saliva. Also, dead skin cells from your inner cheek and tongue. About every three months or so, you digest your own body weight of—you guessed it—you. But you see," she raised a finger, "I'm not a murderer."

"How do you figure?" Sarah asked.

"A homicidal cannibal is someone who kills for food." She wagged that finger. "I don't do that. I don't mind hitting the grocery store once in a while, just like the rest of the human race."

"Then what do you call killing Jacob and his girlfriend, the Rankins and your husband?"

"Survival." She got up from her chair. "But once they're dead, I enjoy them a little longer. Like an airplane crash survivor in a snowy mountainous region. The Donner party. The movie, *Alive*. Getting the picture?" She moved closer. "I practice endocannibalism. This means I consume people from my community. I love me, and I do what's best for me. Always have."

"So you're a narcissistic cannibal because you swallow your own body weight of yourself at least once every three months? Or are you an egotistical cannibal because of so much self-love?"

"Narcissism is such a harsh word, isn't it?" Deborah stopped moving just out of reach. "What's wrong with loving oneself? What's wrong with loving oneself so much that you take the people out of your life who would otherwise harm you?"

"Untie me, and I'll show you how much I love myself and the things I would do to someone who would do me harm."

"Exactly. And because of that, are you narcissistic? How about ego? Isn't the human ego a wonderful thing?"

"Aren't we all ghosts wrapped in a meat suit, made from atoms and particles that comprise everything else in this world?" Sarah asked. "Once the suit's discarded, the spirit moves on. I have nothing to worry about." She pulled on her ankle restraints, harder this time. Her skin tore where the rope had abraded it; blood dripped off her heel.

Luck had come Sarah's way many times. She had never needed to knock on wood, nor had she ever been superstitious. But tied up on a couch and locked in a basement with a homicidal murderer who eats her victims wasn't looking too good.

Was this a test for what Parkman went through as he was forced to his knees while she held a gun to him? Parkman knew her well. He knew she wouldn't pull a weapon on him unless she intended to use it. And yet Parkman didn't beg for his life. She recalled his face and how it calmed at that moment. How he must've felt at that second, knowing it was his last.

Karma can be a whore. What a nasty bitch karma was to turn the scenario around and have Sarah at the precipice, looking over at certain death. Talking to Deborah and waiting her out was only stalling the inevitable. The restraints were so tight she couldn't move. There was no play here, and no one knew where she was.

As Parkman must've felt in those last moments, Sarah felt now.

"I'm sorry, Aaron," Sarah whispered, knowing this was the price she had to pay for betraying her trust. "I'm so sorry, Parkman."

"What was that?" Deborah asked.

Tears streamed down her face as blood dripped from her straining ankles. She had to try to loosen them. She always had to try. Sarah was no quitter.

"I'm sorry for what I did to you …"

"You're sorry for nothing," Deborah shouted. "I'll show you sorry, you stupid, meddling piece of shit!"

Deborah brought her hand out of her pocket, swung her

arm wide, and slammed the side of her fist into Sarah's thigh.

It was so sudden Sarah didn't react. Her reflex, a tiny jerk, only caused her to pull on all the ropes securing her. More blood dripped off her ankles, and her breathing was momentarily choked off.

"What the hell was that?" Sarah screamed as she struggled with her feet, kicking them back and forth.

"Something for the pain." Deborah smiled. It was the kind of smile a clown might use to ignite fear in the children he was about to terrorize at a cannibal county fair.

"What something and what pain?" Sarah asked, already feeling the effects of the drug.

Deborah walked the length of the couch. "You've been such a pain in the ass," she said as she bent out of sight to pick something up. "So I've decided to eat as much of you as I can while doing my best to keep you alive over the coming weeks. How does that sound? You don't have to die right away. Hopefully, you'll be around long enough that your torso will be a stump. Isn't that what you want? To not die right away?"

"Well, kinda, but not on those terms." She couldn't believe she was answering that question so rationally.

She struggled to look the length of the sofa at Deborah, who was now holding something in her hands. Her visionary field wavered, then righted, and she saw what it was.

Deborah held a thick sledgehammer with a long handle.

"Whas … that for?" Sarah managed to get out.

"I always wanted to reenact what Kathy Bates did to James Caan in Stephen King's movie, *Misery*. Did you ever see it? I've always been a big fan of Mr. King. I've read everything."

"Nooo …" Sarah said. But she wasn't sure if it was just a thought or did the words come out.

The sledgehammer rose close to the basement ceiling. When it came down, Deborah swung it sideways.

Sarah felt the blow to her left foot like a freight train had bumped her as it raced past. Then extreme pain shot through her body, contorting her in an awkward position, the ropes pulling on her neck forcefully. Moans came to her from somewhere.

The sledgehammer rose again above Deborah's demonic, evil face. Her eyes were wide and hungry, her lips parted, and her tongue stuck out between them, sluicing back and forth.

The sledgehammer fell.

Sarah's body jerked again.

She was out before the second wave of pain arrived home.

Chapter 28

DETECTIVE COLIN LANG STARED at the ID in his hand and shook his head. Then he examined the papers that authorized the man in front of him to view all their files and do a walkthrough of the crime scene.

"I'm not sure how we can help you." Lang handed the ID back.

"You only need to show me the murder scene. I will examine the files on my own time."

"There have been enough people tramping through that house in the last twenty-four hours; you'd think a frat party had taken place there. What could you see that was any different from what we saw? My best guys are on this."

"I'm merely an observer."

"I don't like this one bit," Lang said, already forgetting the guest's name.

"You don't have to like it. This document isn't a

suggestion. It's an order."

Lang instantly hated this man and his documents. He hated his confidence and his swagger. And he looked like he had just finished a steak dinner with that fucking toothpick in his mouth. Lang had spent some time in Texas over the past decade, where he had heard them call a toothpick a raccoon bone.

"Fine," Lang said to the Raccoon. "We'll take my car."

The detective led the way out of the police building. Once they were in his car and headed toward McKinley Landing, he asked, "Why would they send you all the way up from California?"

"Do you know who Sarah Roberts is?" Raccoon asked.

"A cop-killing homicidal maniac? That about sum it up?"

"Not exactly."

Lang rushed to anger. "What the fuck are you talking about? She rented that house. The mutilated corpse of an RCMP officer was found in her basement after, I might add, she was seen taking that RCMP officer inside the house blindfolded and cuffed. We even have the Jeep she drove with the officer's DNA in the back. There's no doubt."

Raccoon looked out the window.

"Speak," Lang ordered. "What did you mean by not exactly?"

"There's nothing to say. I won't be able to convince you. All you have so far is circumstantial evidence."

"Circumstantial? *Circumstantial?* You want me to turn this car around?" Lang smacked the steering wheel. "Don't sit there all smug and think you know more about this case than I do. I've been interrogating Greg Wright, the guy that entered the Garden of Eden with Sarah and helped her kidnap our mountie. I know more about this case than you know about your own mama."

Raccoon remained quiet, a demure look on his face as he stared out the windshield, chewing a colored toothpick.

"Okay." Lang raised a hand in surrender. "I'll stay calm. We'll view the crime scene together. When we're done, you can report your findings to your superiors in California. I understand procedure. I don't know what you think you'll find at the horror house, but Sarah's long gone. We've checked everywhere. I've got men at each bus depot and train station this side of Katmandu."

"I'm sure you have. The RCMP is doing a fine job."

"Is that sarcasm?"

"Absolutely not."

"Hmmph."

"If the grass is green when you go to bed at night and in the morning when you wake up, there's snow blanketing the yard; you can assume it snowed. The evidence that it snowed is on your grass." Raccoon raised a finger. "But you didn't see it snow because you were sleeping. You didn't *actually* see it fall from the sky. The only proof you have is that the snow is there, covering your grass. That is circumstantial evidence. The circumstances are there, and the evidence is clear, but you didn't witness the act."

"What are you saying? She kidnaps a mountie, ties him up, is seen taking him inside the house he was murdered in, and then she disappears. When we find the mountie's body, you're saying that someone else might have killed him, and we're only assuming Sarah did it? Are you proposing that Sarah didn't do this? Or that our mountie isn't dead?"

"Just keep what I said in mind. Unless you have a

witness who can claim that Sarah killed your mountie, all you have is circumstantial evidence."

Lang drove for a while in silence, afraid he would pull over and shoot the American. But he couldn't hold his silence long. "Why are you here again? Your bosses think we're too close to this?"

"Sarah Roberts is an American citizen. If she has come to Canada to kill cops, we need to know."

"Why's that?"

"Sarah is a valuable American asset. She has done a lot for our country."

"Like what?"

As Lang turned onto McKinley Road, he detected the Raccoon looking at him.

"You didn't take the time to google who you're after?" Raccoon asked.

"It's been one day. We've been doing police work, tracking the perp like we always do. Leg work. Door-to-door stuff. I'm not sitting on a computer playing with a Google."

"Hmmph," Raccoon said.

Now he had a sudden urge to pull the car over and kick the guy's teeth in. The pressure the mounties had been under in the past twenty-four hours had been immense. Losing one of theirs was a tragedy, and it killed something in every member of the force. Guys like his passenger didn't understand that. They rode in on their high horses, examined the evidence, made conclusions, gathered their manila envelopes with their white forms inside, and rode off into the sunset with a few dozen paragraphs written about the life of Lang's friend.

Just like when the mounties took him on fresh out of high

school. He worked in a restaurant in downtown Vancouver. Did the dishes, bused the tables, and finally worked his way up to serving. He developed a hatred for the fellow humans he shared the planet with after serving them food and cleaning up after them for minimum wage. Disgusting idiots and assholes, the whole lot of them. Nothing caused more hatred for the human race than having to clean up after them. Just look at oil spills and nuclear plant meltdowns.

They turned onto Bennett Road. Minutes away now. The sooner he got rid of this meddling American, the better.

"Detective Lang?"

"Yeah?" His tone was harsher than he meant it to be.

"Would you agree what Hitler did was horrible?"

"What? What is this? How does that have anything to do with the murder of Barry Ashford? Now we're talking about World War II?"

"Just answer the question. Humor me."

It grated on his nerves that his guest never changed the sound of his voice. No inflection. Just monotone the whole time, like Steven Wright, the comedian.

"Yes, what Hitler did was horrible."

A police cruiser was coming their way. Lang rolled his window down. The cruiser came even with them and stopped.

"Where are you headed?" Lang asked the uniform.

"Off-site."

"Why?"

"Was called off. Apparently, by special request of Mrs. Ashford. She wants to grieve without the constant reminder of us at her front door."

"And this was authorized?" Lang asked.

"Yeah, strange, but it was."

"The murder house still open?"

"Yellow taped but open."

"Fine." Lang pulled away. "What was that about Hitler?" he asked the raccoon bone man.

"In 1894, a priest saved a four-year-old boy from drowning. That boy's name was Adolf Hitler."

"So?"

"Don't you find that ironic? A man of God saved one of the greatest murderers of our time?"

Lang slowed his unmarked cruiser two houses short of Deborah Ashford's home so she wouldn't see the car. If she wanted officers off her street for a while, the last thing he wanted to do was park right in front. She deserved all the respect the mounties could offer her in her time of loss and grief.

"How has that got anything to do with this scenario?" Lang angled sideways in the seat to face his guest, who was turning out to be some kind of enigmatic lunatic.

"Think about it." The guest opened his door and stopped. "The thing to focus on was the priest, the man of God." He looked back at Lang. "When you do your research, you'll see who Sarah is and why she was here. Maybe then you won't be so blinded by anger and revenge."

It was good that his American guest got out of the car because Lang had the urge to shoot him.

"Who the fuck do you think you are?" Lang whispered to the empty car.

He followed the Raccoon to the front door of the house. The American stood on the front stoop and looked inside for a few seconds. Then he closed his eyes, took a deep breath, let it out slowly, and opened his eyes.

Lang frowned. "What the hell are you doing?"

"Taking everything in. If our killer walked across this threshold, I want to feel everything they felt and do everything they did. I must walk the crime scene and deduce what I can, organizing everything in a mental filing cabinet. You okay with that?"

"Whatever."

"You're angry with me?" Raccoon asked, turning to face Lang.

"I'm angry at the whole situation. Cops shouldn't be shot and cut to pieces."

"Can I ask you something?"

"What?"

"What was Barry Ashford doing associated with a place like the Garden of Eden? Wasn't there a conflict of interest somewhere in there?"

Lang frowned. "Are you kidding? Ashford was killed and cut up, and you're wondering why he owned a small business on the side?"

"You're right. Forget about it."

"No, I will not forget about it." Lang shot past him and entered the house, bumping Raccoon's shoulder as he went by. He stopped in the kitchen. "Do this walkthrough thing. Then I take you back, and you can leave my city."

Raccoon moved by him, taking the kitchen in, staring at counters, touching them, and looking over at the living room.

"It just seems like a risqué kind of business to own for a decorated police officer."

"Would you stop with the trashing Barry shit," Lang yelled, his temper on a thin piece of string ready to snap. "He was a good guy. He was *one* of the guys. Wouldn't hurt a fly. And in Canada, it's legal to have a massage parlor. They license those things. They even struck down the prostitution laws a while back. It's legal for private citizens to do what they want within the confines of the law. Fucking bawdy houses are opening up in all the major cities across Canada. What Barry Ashford was doing was child's play compared to some out there. Now get off his back."

Raccoon didn't blink, flinch, or even crack a smile. Cool as a cucumber, his guest moved by him, turned at the top of the stairs, and stopped.

"That thing you're feeling on the inside," the guest fluttered his hand near his solar plexus. "That pain in the gut isn't because of something I said, and it's not grief. It's the part of your mind," he touched his temple with his finger, "that agrees with me. You're offended by the truth. It's okay, though. You're not alone. Everyone does it."

Lang stood open-mouthed as the man walked down the stairs.

"Why do I get all the shit jobs?" Lang asked himself. "Taxiing this asshole around."

He followed the American down the stairs and kept an eye on him as he examined the crime scene. The man walked by the metal chair that once held Lang's colleague and friend, leaned down, and looked at the light that was angled toward the chair. He checked the rolled-up carpet on the side of the room. Raccoon walked circles around the death chair until he stopped by the window. The sun shone behind the man with the toothpick. He paid the view of the lake behind him, with the two water skiers no attention. Instead, he stared at the far wall.

He got down and knelt by the window. Lang waited. When Raccoon rose to stand, he walked to the wall behind the big floor light and opened the closet.

Lang watched as the American looked at the clock on the wall, behind it, and back at the clock.

"What?" Lang asked.

"What time is it?"

Lang checked his watch. "Ten after two in the afternoon."

"Right."

"So the clock's batteries are dead. Who cares?"

"This isn't only a clock."

"Looks like it from here."

"That's what she was betting on."

Lang moved closer. He leaned around the edge of the closet and peeked inside. A VCR-like machine sat on the top shelf of a cabinet. A green light blinked in the far corner.

"What is it?"

"The clock is a camera, and this is a DVR. Sarah wouldn't go to all this trouble to interrogate an RCMP officer without recording what she would discover."

"How come none of my officers saw this? And how do you know she was interrogating our mountie?"

Raccoon met his eyes. "You can't see that by the way this room is set up?"

"I thought this was to torture him."

"That might have been Sarah's plan as well. Whoever killed Barry Ashford, and I suspect Barry himself, didn't see this clock/camera either. The murderer will be in full living color on the hard drive of this DVR. Once we've watched it, you will learn who you really should be hunting."

Lang breathed a heavy sigh, unsure if he could watch Barry be shot and cut up.

"There's a TV upstairs," Raccoon said. He twitched his toothpick to the other side of his mouth. "Let's go see who killed your mountie, shall we?"

For the first time since Detective Lang met the American, he actually sounded happy.

Chapter 29

DEBORAH CHECKED THROUGH THE curtains one more time. The street was still empty. She made room in the Rankins' freezer, shifting around some of the meat from Jacob and his girlfriend.

She laughed. If Barry had known what she had been feeding him for the past several months, he would've killed her instead of the other way around. Barry's thighs and calves were still in her bathtub in her basement. They would need to be tended to before they began to decay. Now that the authorities were gone, she could bring his legs over undetected so she could skin and clean the meat and package it for consumption.

But she wanted to deal with Sarah first. There would be time enough to bring Barry's legs over later tonight. With Sarah, she wanted to start slow, cut small pieces of meat out, and cook and eat her flesh right in front of her. Breaking her left ankle would help when she sawed the foot off. Cutting through bone was always tough, but broken ankles allowed the feet to almost lop off as the blade bypassed the bones.

She considered cutting out Sarah's tongue first so there would be no more disrespect, no more talking back.

Sure, she thought of everything, she got the blowtorch ready to cauterize the wound as she cut through Sarah's flesh.

If Deborah made a mistake, Sarah would die. But that wasn't so bad. It would be more merciful for Sarah, but Debbie wouldn't enjoy it as much.

She checked the curtains one more time because she couldn't have someone too close to the house in case Sarah fought through the drugs and woke screaming with the pain.

The street was still empty.

It was time to cut her meat for dinner. She turned on the Bosch all-purpose electric saw, the blade cutting the air back and forth, and walked over to Sarah's unconscious body and hovered near her ankle.

An eerie feeling coursed through her. Like she was being watched.

She turned off the saw and eyed the curtains. She looked over each shoulder but saw nothing. She was alone with Sarah.

When she looked back down, Sarah's eyes were open.

"You're awake?" Deborah exclaimed, stepping back. The anesthetic she used should have knocked Sarah out as if she was on the cardiac specialist's table awaiting a heart transplant. "How is that possible?"

Deborah pulled the syringe from her pocket. All its contents had been injected into Sarah's thigh. There was no way Sarah could be awake.

When she turned back to look at the young girl's face, there was something different about her. The eyes, her jaw, her cheeks, something. But she couldn't put a finger on it.

"Deborah Sally Ashford, nee Cummings." The voice emanating from Sarah was cryptic, almost hollow like she was speaking through a tin can with a string attached. The kind kids used as pretend phones years ago.

Deborah gasped. "How did you know my whole name? And my maiden name?"

"I know … *everything*." The first two words were the tin can again, but the last word sounded malevolent.

Goosebumps raised on Deborah's arms.

"You have enough narcotics in your system to put down a charging bull," Deborah said, her voice wavering at the sight of Sarah's glaring eyes. "Your left foot is broken. How is it possible you're talking? And in that weird voice?"

"This is the end, Deb Head."

"Don't call me that!" she shouted.

"Deb Head, Deb Head, Deb Head …"

Deborah dropped the electric saw and clapped both hands over her ears. That name brought her back to when she was a teenager. Her mother would beat her with a broom, always yelling that Deborah wasn't thinking. Her mother would say, *Deb, you have to use your head. How stupid are you? Deb has a head. Come on, Deb Head. What is wrong with you? Why are you such a stupid child? How could I have a dumb idiot for a kid? Come on, Deb, use your head. Deb Head. You're so stupid, you brainless piece of shit.* With each exclamation, the broom would come down on her back. Her ribs were broken at least a dozen times before she left home and ran to Vancouver at fifteen.

"Did Deb Head want to talk about Vancouver?" the thing on Rankins's sofa asked.

Deborah swiveled her head back and forth slowly. "You're not real, you're not real," she said repeatedly. "You can't know my name. You can't know about me. No one knows about my past. No one knows that name—"

"I know," Sarah's body said, the voice worsening, more strained. "What you did to Maxine's eyes. You kept them in that jar and toyed with the idea that you would find a way to serve them to your husband mashed up in his food. I'm here to stop you."

Deborah looked at the saw. If the thing on the sofa didn't shut up, she would cut its head off. Whatever Sarah had become, Debbie Ashford would un-become it.

"You can't stop me with that," the Sarah thing said. "I know what you're thinking as you think it."

The thing on the couch moved. Sarah raised her hands and slipped her finger under the rope wrapped around her neck. She pulled hard on her feet, making the rope as taut as it could possibly be. Then, with a sudden jerk that no person could rationally do because of the pain, Sarah pulled her broken foot forward, straining the rope to its end. Because her ankle was loose and broken, no longer in a fixed position, Sarah snapped her knee back, and her left foot popped out of the restraints. The effect timed perfectly, yanking the rope off her left foot. She repeated the movement quicker now that one foot was free and freed the other as the rope snapped the couch's leg under it. What Deborah thought was impossible, the thing on the couch performed with ease.

Next, Sarah gave a serious yank on the rope around her neck, and both couch legs at that end popped from under the couch, the sofa dropping several inches with a thump. The rope around her neck fell loosely to the sofa's cushion.

Sarah was no longer secured but couldn't walk away with one broken ankle.

Deborah grabbed the electric saw, sweat dripping into her eyes, and turned it on.

"I will cut you up!" she screamed, lunging forward.

Sarah rolled off the couch as the electric saw came at her. It sank deep into the middle cushion when Sarah hit the carpet and rolled into Deborah's legs.

The sharpest pain Deborah had ever felt shot up her leg as if a wasp the size of a football stung her. Forgetting the electric saw, she looked down. Blood ran freely from a wound in her leg where Sarah had just bit her.

"How does it feel?" the Sarah thing asked. "You like being eaten alive?"

"This isn't happening," Deborah wailed. "You're still unconscious. You're still my prisoner. How did you get untied? This doesn't make sense. No one can …" She stopped rambling and dropped to the floor as her leg weakened.

Sarah was crawling onto the couch.

"Who are you?" Deborah asked.

The saw turned on.

Sarah hovered near her, the electric saw in her hands, balancing crazily on her knees, her broken left foot flopping behind her like an afterthought.

"No one can handle that kind of pain," Deborah said.

"Sarah's not feeling anything right now," the voice said.

Deborah's eyes widened, sure she had lost her mind. She backed away from the Sarah thing.

"Who are you?" Deborah shouted.

"My name is Vivian Roberts."

Deborah screamed.

Chapter 30

Lang pushed the rewind button. "I have to see it again. That's just not possible."

"What am I missing?" Raccoon asked. "It's as clear as day."

Lang watched again as Sarah interrogated Barry. Officer Ashford admitted to abusing his girls. Then Sarah left the basement. The lights went out. The camera turned off. Movement activated it again. The lights were on. Barry's head moved. Finally, someone walked onto the screen. A woman. She talked to Barry. Lang recognized Deborah's voice. Enough of her face showed to prove it was Barry's wife. She held a gun in her hand. When she used it to shoot Barry, Lang gasped again. Deborah grabbed a saw and proceeded to dismember him on camera. After a few minutes, she disappeared and returned with an ax to finish her work. It was Deborah Ashford who murdered her husband. It was plain to see, clear as day.

"Do you have any idea where this woman is right now?" Raccoon asked.

Lang was stunned into silence.

Fingers snapped in front of his face.

He jumped. "What?"

"That officer we talked to as we arrived," Raccoon was talking again. "He said he was called off by the widow. Is that the widow?"

Detective Colin Lang nodded as if in a trance.

"She lives next door?"

Lang continued to nod.

The American guest spit his toothpick out and pulled out a weapon as he ran toward the front door. Lang snapped out of his trance and spun on his heels.

"Hey, wait," he yelled.

But his American guest was gone.

Detective Lang ran across the floor and outside just in time to see the American vault up the front steps to the Ashford house and body-check the door.

"Hey!" he yelled as he ran across the lawn. "We have to do this right."

The American smashed the door three times before Lang caught up to him. The American broke through as he hit the stairs, the door snapping off at the handle.

He entered, his gun raised. "Mrs. Ashford," the American called. "Police."

He ran away from Lang, checking rooms down the hall to the left. Lang moved into the kitchen. Nothing seemed out of the ordinary.

The American rushed past him and whispered, "All clear

up here."

"What are you doing?" Lang asked. "There are procedures. We need to get a warrant. We need to make—"

The most emotion the American had shown since Lang met him was on his face. His eyes were on fire; his cheeks moistened in sweat. "Do you know where Sarah Roberts is?"

Lang shook his head in the negative.

"We've got a murderer out there. Sarah's BMW bike was found in a ditch, and her rental car was found just up the street. That means she's probably close. Find the widow, your murderer; find Sarah."

The American disappeared down the stairs.

Lang didn't feel comfortable standing in Barry Ashford's house. Even though he witnessed the murder on the DVR, it somehow felt disrespectful to the widow to just be standing there. Lang pulled out his cell phone. He stepped outside and called for backup. Backup would arrive very soon.

That's when he heard someone scream from far away. It wasn't in the house behind him. It was from somewhere in the trees beyond the dead-end road.

The scream came again.

Then someone bumped into him from behind.

The American was back. He had paled in the time he was in the basement.

"I found his legs in the bathtub downstairs." He panted a moment, trying to catch his breath. "Barry's wife placed his fucking legs in her tub as if they were a macabre trophy!"

The scream came once more.

The American jerked his head to the side. "Did you hear that?"

Lang nodded. "It was the third or fourth time."

The American took off running, pumping his arms like he was trying to set a hundred-meter dash record.

Chapter 31

The Bosch electric saw touched the edge of Deborah's neck but didn't go farther. The wind from the blade tickled her skin.

Sarah moved in until they were nose to nose.

"You will pay," Sarah's mouth said in that terrible voice. "For what you have done."

Sarah jerked the electric saw until the cord snapped out of the wall. The saw turned off.

She sat it beside Deborah, rolled off her, and lay back. Silence filled the room.

"What are you doing?" Deborah asked.

"Waiting …" Sarah's eyes stayed open a moment longer. Then, as her eyes closed and without moving her lips, she said, "Waiting for them."

Her eyes closed, and her head tilted to the side as if she had lost consciousness.

A siren wailed in the distance. More sirens joined.

Deborah wondered if anyone had heard them screaming and called the police.

She got to her feet on shaky legs, keeping an eye on Sarah's inert form the whole time. She teetered to the window and pulled the curtains back. Police cruisers were just turning onto Bennett Road at the end. Lights flashed, and sirens screamed. One cruiser after another came barreling down the street.

She had to use another hypodermic. Keep Sarah subdued. She had to get out of there and clean up in her home. No one could see her in this house. If they ever searched it, they would find meat supplies—the remains of more than a dozen people.

But something else was wrong. Why would all these police cruisers be on her street? One maybe. But twelve or more and with their sirens on?

She brushed at her hair and straightened her clothes. There was an extra needle in the laundry room. She gave Sarah's sleeping form a wide berth as she headed there.

When she came out, the needle in her hand, ready to inject Sarah, two men stood by the couch. They both held guns pointed at her. She recognized Lang from afternoon barbecues and get-togethers at various police functions.

This didn't look good. A story formed in her head so fast it surprised her.

"I'm so happy you're here," Deborah said. "I came over to get this house ready for a cleaning when I discovered her." She pointed at Sarah on the floor. "The murderer that killed my husband. We fought. I got lucky and broke her ankle. She passed out, and I was about to give her a little something," she held the needle up, "to keep her asleep until I got back from calling you lot. But it sounds like you're all here. It's so good to see you, Colin."

"Put the needle down, Deborah," Lang said.

"Okay, okay, no need to be rude about it. Just trying to secure a murderer."

"Step away from the needle and put your hands on the wall."

"Colin, what are you saying? It's me you're talking to. Deborah Ashford, Barry's widow—"

"Don't mention his name!" Colin smacked the needle from her hand, twisted her around, and pushed her against the wall. "Hands on your head."

One of her arms was wrenched down, and something cold and metallic slammed onto it. The other followed.

"You are under arrest for the murder of RCMP Officer Barry Ashford."

But his voice faded for her. She was watching as the other man bent down and tended to Sarah. He examined her feet and then lifted her eyelids.

The man was crying.

How odd.

Lang shoved her through the door and into the sunlight.

It was over. She had no idea how they found out, but it was over. Even though she had covered all her bases and was sure they had nothing on her, she knew this was it.

Maybe in jail, she would become a vegetarian.

That would really fuck with their heads.

Chapter 32

When Sarah woke in the hospital, they had already operated on her foot. They added titanium plates and screws to help mend the bones. It would take months, but she'd be able to walk again. Until then, she would have to learn how to use crutches.

She had given her statements to the police, which took up most of the first two days she was awake. She explained to the police that her main focus was getting Lesley out of the Garden of Eden. When Greg tried unsuccessfully to remove her from the premises, they went back together.

Sarah abducted Barry Ashford so she could secretly record his confession. She had no idea that Deborah would kill him, just as she had no idea that Deborah would try to kill her. She had assumed Barry was the threat.

Detective Colin Lang had asked what possessed her to think she could abduct a member of the RCMP without consequences. She felt Barry's confession would be enough for any jury to let her walk. After all, the man was committing heinous crimes against the female employees of the Garden of Eden.

The massage parlor had closed down. The city revoked their license and refused to issue a new one.

Greg and Lesley had come by to visit. They brought flowers. Lesley thanked her for saving her life, and Greg thanked her for everything else. During their visit, Sarah had teared up as the room filled with emotion. Lesley would soon be heading to rehab, where she would get the help she needed.

Sarah talked to her mother and reassured her everything was okay. Aaron had called, too. They planned a reunion at her house in Santa Rosa, where she would recuperate with her parents.

Exhausted, weak, and ready to sleep, she lowered her electric bed, swiveled the food tray to the side, and laid her head on the pillow.

Her door opened.

"Yes?" she said.

No one answered.

She opened her sleepy eyes and lifted her head.

Parkman.

"What are you doing here?" she asked, her voice soft, not angry.

"I think it's about time we talked about what happened in Santa Rosa."

He closed the door and headed for the chair beside the bed.

"Parkman, there's nothing to talk about. I pulled a gun

and was about to shoot you for something you didn't do. Even when I had the evidence in my head, had I taken the time to think about it, I would've known it wasn't you." She cleared her throat. "In my mind, some things are unforgivable. What I did to you falls in that category."

"Are you willing to consider that you were suffering from a head wound? You don't think that had anything to do with your confusion?"

She turned away to hide her pain. She didn't deserve his friendship, his love. Her single act had made her unworthy of him.

"I can hear you," he said.

"What?" She looked at him.

"Inside, you're fighting yourself, and it doesn't matter if you win or lose because, in the end, you'll lose."

"What are you talking about?"

"You and I have known each other for years. I'm pretty sure I'm the only one in law enforcement you trust. We've been through a lot together and covered each other's backs. But you made one mistake and called it quits. That doesn't sum you up. You're different." He leaned forward and rested his elbows on his thighs. "So tell me, what's really going on?"

"I almost killed you, Parkman. I don't deserve people in my life when I'm a danger to them."

"Are you a danger to me?"

"Well, no, not now."

He leaned back in his chair. "What do I have to do to get you back? We have history together. I won't let that fall away because you're upset about a little gunplay."

"It wasn't a little gunplay, and you know it."

"Sarah, this seems unreasonable. And it seems that it's more about you than me. Why are you hurting yourself this way?"

"It's what I deserve. For what I did."

"You didn't *do* anything."

"You don't understand, Parkman. To see that image in my mind." She wiped at the tears tickling her cheek. She hated to cry but couldn't help this one. "And to think you betrayed me. To want to hurt you. Those were black heart days. Then to find out you were trying to save me." She covered her face with her hands. "I was devastated at what I did. I am devastated."

"Then let me help you," he said. "What would've happened had Detective Lang and I not shown up at that house?"

"I don't know. I was knocked out."

"No. According to Mrs. Ashford, you were not knocked out. She claims you woke up and said your name was Vivian. But forget that for a minute. I came for you. I pulled a lot of strings to get a look at that murder scene. Let's say I saved your life. Now you owe me. How's that? You have to come back. You have to let me back in. Deal?"

Her hands still over her face, she heard the pain in his voice.

Then he was moving. His arms wrapped around her. They tightened. She shuddered. They cried together.

After a few minutes, he released her.

"I'm so sorry, Parkman."

"I know you are, and so am I."

He grabbed a Kleenex box and handed her some. After wiping her face, she pulled a notebook from under her pillow.

"Here."

"What's this?"

"Read it. You'll know."

Parkman read the first few pages fast, then looked up.

"Vivian really did this?"

Sarah nodded. "Unbelievable, isn't it?"

"Wow. I had no idea she could."

"Neither did I. The drugs incapacitated me. But nothing man-made can incapacitate Vivian. She said it was a struggle to channel through me, but it was easier as I wasn't fighting against her."

"How did she let it get so far? If we didn't show up when we did, you could've been killed or worse."

"I suspect Vivian let it go that far because she knew you were coming. She wanted us to be close again and allowing you to find me … well, maybe it was her way of fixing us."

"If that's the case, then I'm happy you were stuck in that basement." He smiled. "You almost dying at the hands of a cannibal turns out to be a good thing."

"Gee, thanks."

"There's something else."

"What?"

"Some colleagues of mine are having a problem."

"What kind of problem?"

"Dead bodies."

"I can see how that would be a problem. Are you going to tell me more?"

"Will you help?"

"On that much information?"

He shook his head. "No, Sarah. I want to know if telling you is a waste of time. Will you be willing to help me? This could be a chance to clean whatever stain you've allowed on your soul."

She dabbed at the last of the tears on her cheeks. He was right. This was a chance to do something for Parkman. To redeem herself with him. To make things right, even though it felt like their fences were already mended.

"Will I be working with you?"

"Almost the whole time."

"Then I'm in. One hundred percent. I want to redeem myself with you."

"That's not what this is about."

"It is now. Tell me more."

"In and around Los Angeles, the Catholic Church has had four priests murdered. There's a threat that more murders will take place. The police have nothing to go on. One of their sergeants is an old friend of mine, David Hirst. He knows about you and asked if we would be interested in looking at the case."

"You mean you want me to become some kind of psychic detective? You want me to help the police? The very people I don't trust and who I just spent the greater part of last week antagonizing?"

"That's exactly what I want." He crossed his arms and stared down at her.

"Then I'll do it. It'll allow me to redeem myself with the police forces who heard of my involvement here. I don't want itchy fingers on guns wherever I go because they didn't hear the whole story. If I can do something good in Los Angeles, then I will. Call Aaron. Tell him we're not going to Santa Rosa. We're on our way to Los Angeles. See if he can join me there. When do we start?"

"As soon as you're fit to travel."

"Get me crutches. We'll leave now. Grab my clothes in that closet."

"You just had your foot set. You can't leave yet."

"Parkman, when have you ever seen me overstay my welcome in a hospital? Maybe I'll need a wheelchair, or maybe I'll hop on one foot down the hall, but I'm leaving today. Let's do this. I want to be a psychic detective. I want to help the police this time. I want to redeem my name with them and with you. I want to be *The Redeemed*. Grab me my fucking clothes, and let's go save the priests. I need to make this right with you. There will be no more shit between us, or I'll kill both of us."

Without another word, Parkman grabbed her clothes.

Afterword

Dear Reader,

I make it a habit to maintain a buy-a-cop-a-coffee campaign. Whenever I find myself in a Starbucks, or some other coffee shop, where I see a uniformed officer or a fireman, I take it upon myself to head over to the counter and buy their coffee.

I bought three firemen their lunch in a Subway Sandwich Shop.

I don't do it because I want a thank you or any kind of praise. I do it to say thank you. I do it to praise the work these emergency services members do every time they don their uniforms. These hard-working men and women go to work and risk their lives every day. The least we could do is say thank you.

I'll never forget how I watched in horror as the towers fell that fateful day in New York on a sunny September morning. All those lives lost. The firemen ran inside the building. The police officers followed them in.

I'm still moved to silence.

I write about bad cops. I hurt bad cops. I have rogue cops murdered in my book in the worst possible way. I do this because they're not just bad or rogue. They're disgusting. Mind you, this is just my opinion, but when authorities break bad, they don't just disgrace the uniform, they disgrace the name of every officer and every fireman who has died in the line of duty. Every emergency services employee that has ever died trying to carry a child out of a burning building. Every cop who was shot after pulling a car over. Every single one of them has been disrespected when a cop goes bad, and I despise that.

So for fictional purposes, I wanted to write about Barry Ashford because Kelowna, the gorgeous city that it is, has bad cops.

The Buddy Tavares story in the novel was true. The RCMP officer kicked him in the face when he was already down and got off lightly. This officer was suspected of other cases of violence while on duty, but that's another story.

Watch the video here,

http://www.youtube.com/watch?v=hiFjz0PSckg

In addition to that touchy subject, I wanted to explore what Sarah is going through after the previous novel, *Killing Sarah*. I think some of us sometimes do a little self-loathing for the decisions we've made and then make new decisions that sabotage us. Sarah has issues to work through, but in this novel, she needed to be alone and just work with Vivian and get a lot of anger off her chest. Coming to Kelowna to deal with Barry helped her. Seeing what Parkman went through firsthand while knowing she would probably die in the Rankins' basement gave her a new perspective on life and a new look at her relationships.

Now that Sarah and Parkman are back, they will be on a wild ride in *The Redeemed*, Sarah Roberts Book Eleven.

She will redeem herself with him, with police forces worldwide, and with Aaron. By the time we get to the next book, *The Haunted*, Sarah Roberts Book Twelve, she will just have memories of these days. Memories that will haunt her. And then we get to *The Unlucky*, Sarah Roberts Book Thirteen. Well, you'll have to wait and see just how unlucky Sarah gets in that one. It's a ride that doesn't bode well for Sarah, but I think she'll be up for it. Maybe, just maybe …

Until then, thanks for reading, as always. I do this for you. Without you, I couldn't do this. That's why I love you all.

Forever yours,
Jonas Saul

About Jonas Saul

Jonas Saul is the bestselling author of the Sarah Roberts Series—more than two million sold!—and has written and published over sixty thrillers. After acquiring an agent, he signed several deals in Los Angeles, with MadRiver Pictures optioning his Sarah Roberts Series— over forty books!—(currently in development).

Jonas has often outranked Stephen King and Dean

Koontz on Amazon over the past decade. He's regularly invited to be a guest speaker, teacher, or workshop presenter at international writing conferences and film festivals worldwide. He hosts an annual writer's retreat in Greece, where he currently lives. He focuses his teaching on how to get tension and emotion in every scene, on every page, how he made it as a creator/writer, the path to success in this business, and the pitfalls to avoid. He also hosts a reading retreat in Greece with guest authors, yoga retreats, and hiking retreats. Visit the Imagine Greece Retreats website at www.imaginegreeceretreats.com, or email him directly to discuss an opportunity to join one of the retreats at jonas@imaginegreeceretreats.com.

Jonas is also a professional freelance editor. He works for several publishers and does private editing for clients, with many testimonials on his website at www.imaginepress.org, which details each author's response to Jonas's editing skills. Email Jonas directly for an editing quote at editor@imaginepress.org.

To book Jonas for a speaking engagement at a writer's conference/festival, to have him on your jury at a film festival, or even to say hello, email Jonas directly at jonassaul@icloud.com.

For updates on releases, hit the "Follow" button on Amazon or Bookbub, and join Jonas on Facebook, where he's most active.

Contact Jonas Saul

Linktree: Find me here

Email: jonassaul@icloud.com

9 781998 047093